SULTRY SEATTLE NIGHTS

BROTHERHOOD PROTECTORS WORLD

PAIGE YANCEY

Twisted Page Press LLC

BROTHERHOOD PROTECTORS

ORIGINAL SERIES BY ELLE JAMES

PROLOGUE

THE BLARING sound of the medical transport bus was heard coming down the road that passed by the hospital. The wind picked up; a few wisps of hair escaped her military regulation bun and whipped around her face. Amongst the dark sky, stars a bright full moon shone around the large storm clouds that were forming. The medical transport bus normally did not arrive this early in the morning, but her surgical team was always prepared when they received the call. From behind the bus sped along a military jeep. Four large men in bulky gear jumped from the dark vehicle and parked across from the hospital entrance. They walked up to stand with her team. The bus came to a stop and medical support crew came from the front entrance to help with stretchers, and moved the military injured into the hospital for surgery or recovery. The Landstuhl Regional Medical Center a military hospital in Germany is the go between for injured military personnel from Afghanistan and Iraq.

Dr. Siobhan Monahan ran forward, her white coat kicking up as she moved. She was waved forward to assess a patient who would need surgical care, her stethoscope bell in her hand as she placed the ear tips in her ears. She leaned over the stretcher, noticing from the corner of her eyes that the soldiers that had stopped in the vehicle from the parking area had formed ranks around her and the patient. Putting the bell over his chest, she listened for a pulse. The man on the gurney had a low heart rate and shallow breathing.

One of the medical personnel with him turned toward her while they still moved in unison to carry the gurney forward. "His vitals have been dropping for the last hour."

From her left one of the men spoke and from the lights of the hospital she could see his crystal blue eyes.

"He was shot by an insurgent when we were on a mission. I patched him up, and we were on the helo within 30 minutes to the forward location surgical team near us in Afghanistan."

They moved through the lit entrance of the surgical area. The building was usually quiet at this time of morning. Her medical unit had received a call that an incoming special ops team was escorting in one of their own, and they were to prep for surgery. She'd been napping on one of the cots set aside for the docs on call.

Moving as one, they entered through sliding glass doors, and her team of doctors and nurses swarmed the patient to start setting up IVs and prep for surgery. Out of the corner of her eye, she could see the four men step back, but all stood in protective stances around the medical team. Her team had their comrade on a mobile medical bed and were swiftly moving down the hallway. Siobhan began shouting orders to her staff as they quickly ran with her down the hallway.

"Ma'am?" Mr. Blue Eyes looked at her. His arms where crossed over his chest.

"Please wait in the surgical floor waiting room. We're going straight into surgery; it will be a few hours."

The surgery for their team member took more hours than she liked to count, and they almost lost the patient twice, but finally, he pulled through. He had been stabilized from injuries due to an IED, but the wounds to his torso had been severe including shrapnel that had been embedded internally that they needed a more refined surgical team to work on. Her nurses settled him into the ICU, and she went to talk to his team. Pulling off the surgical cover that had been holding her hair out of her face, she walked into the floor's waiting area. The blond man with the bright blue eyes walked up to her and extended his hand. Both shook, and she noticed his grip was almost punishing.

"My name is J.B. Wayne but everyone calls me Atlas."

"Nice to meet you, Atlas. My name is Dr. Monahan. I just wanted to let you gentlemen know your friend is in stable condition but not out of the woods, yet. The shrapnel that was embedded in his chest had severed several major arteries and the bleeding was extensive. We had to remove his gallbladder and part of his left lung, but all other organs are still intact, and the arteries stitched up. We'll keep him for observation for a few days."

All the men nodded, and the large man beside Atlas said, "Thank you, ma'am."

"Do you guys have any questions?" Each of them

shook his head. "Alright make sure you give the charge nurse a good contact number." With a quick about-face, she turned to leave. Her shift had finished hours ago, and she was ready to head to her quarters.

Even though she was tired, she rushed to the locker room, took a quick warm shower and brushed out her hair. Out of the bun, her hair was long and halfway down her back. After blow-drying it, she glanced into the mirror with steam around its edges. She pulled on soft faded blue jeans, a white button-up blouse, and low, brown leather boots. As she hustled out of the locker room, she grabbed her go bag and a navy-blue blazer. With sure steps, she walked toward the front entrance to head to her car. To the side of the entrance, with his arm leaning against the wall stood Blue Eyes. *No, his name is, J.B. Wayne—Atlas.* Glancing at his large frame, she noticed that his call sign seemed to suit him much better than his birth name.

He pushed away from the wall, and she noticed that his arms had bulging muscles, his waist was slim, and through his jeans, his thighs and calves were thick with corded muscles. Distracted by the way his legs moved, she didn't realize that he'd spoken to her until he cleared his throat.

Looking up into his eyes, she asked him, "I'm sorry what did you say?"

His eyes seemed to sparkle, and a little grin formed on his lips. "As a thank you, I'd like to take you out for a drink; it's kind of a custom the boys have after we have completed a mission. The rest of the guys went on their own, and Davie Boy is here, I thought you could be his stand in."

"Oh, I couldn't," she sputtered.

She was an officer in the Army and a doctor this request was out of the ordinary. Doctors did not go for drinks with their patients, or their family or friends. As an officer she wasn't to mix ranks with enlisted and being that he was an officer as well, it didn't go against that rule. Her hesitation must have shown because he moved in next to her.

"I know my request is unusual, but I figured a couple drinks wouldn't hurt especially since you are off duty. Also, we are leaving for the States tomorrow and we are getting new orders once we get back home."

He placed his large hand under her elbow and started to lead her out the door. Because of the warmth of his hand and his gentle persistence, she went along with him. The cool air outside the hospital didn't seem to affect her, likely because the heat of his palm where he touched her radiated up her arm and warmed her deep inside. Just as she started to come out of the warm fuzzy feeling, she realized that they were walking up to a taxi.

"Here, let me get the door for you."

He let go of her arm and stepped forward to open the door. Once he let go of her arm, she suddenly felt the cool air and was tired again. Atlas turned back to her, took her elbow and helped her inside the vehicle. Once she was safely seated he shut the door, and then jogged around to the other side and hopped in.

"I've been here a few times, so I know of a few good bars. Is there one you prefer?"

"I know a good place out of the way of normal traffic, and they have food too." To the driver, she spoke German, "Just head out of the base and go left."

She directed the taxi driver to the bar, and once they arrived, Atlas came around again and opened her door. He paid the driver, and together, they walked toward the entrance of the bar. The night was dark, and the building was also a dull dark color. A large blinking sign on the outside, with several of the letters missing, was blinking, casting a reddish light.

Again, Atlas opened the door for her, and the sound of a guitar could be heard inside. This was a folksy type bar, not like the loud colorful techno clubs that were so popular in Germany. Walking toward the long, wooden bar, she took a stool and he sat down next to her.

"What's your poison?" he asked with a grin.

"I'm simple. A Guinness." She smiled back.

Turning and motioning to the bartender, he looked at her to make the order in German. The server returned to them with their drinks and they both took sips from them.

With a wink, he smiled down at her. "Aww that is so much better than Tang in dirt water."

She noticed that he sat several inches taller than her, and his legs where flat on the ground, while her feet were hooked into the last rung of the stool.

"So, Doc, where are you from?"

"You can call me Siobhan, and I'm originally from Seattle."

"I like that name. What is it—Irish?"

"My family has a strong Irish background, and since I was born with red hair, my mom and dad thought it was fitting. How about you, where are you from?"

"I'm really from all over. My dad was in the Air

Force growing up and my brothers, mom, and I moved a lot."

Another set of Guinness's were placed in front of them, and since she enjoyed his company and the drink, she set in to drink this one as well. Time seemed to have no meaning as they talked about their families and careers, laughing about the adventures they'd both had. Realizing how late it was getting, Siobhan went to stand, wobbled, and almost fell over. The bar seemed to be spinning, but suddenly a strong arm came around her waist and scooped her against a muscular body. Atlas looked down into her eyes, and his face seemed to be very close.

"Doc, I've been wanting to do this since I first saw you; do I have your permission to give you a kiss?" She nodded yes and licked her lips; his face seemed to move quickly, and then his mouth was on hers.

She inhaled his deep masculine scent and breathed him in as his mouth devoured hers. A large hand cupped her butt, and her hips were pressed firmly into his. She wrapped her arms around his neck and held on for dear life. No thoughts seemed to want to form, but she heard someone say behind them that their taxi was here.

The kiss broke, and they both gasped for air. He didn't let go of her waist but turned her around and led her out of the bar toward a waiting taxi. He helped her in, and then scooted in beside her not letting go of her through the whole process.

Leaning carefully forward she gave the driver her address, and he started forward with a lurch. She sprawled back into Atlas's arms and leaned toward his mouth. The kiss lasted the short distance to her apartment, and he helped her out of the taxi and up to her door. Once at her door, the world seemed to spin, and he took the keys and opened her door. With a slow turn, she looked up into his eyes and said, "I think you're going to spend the night with me."

Then she grabbed the sides of his shirt collar and pulled him down for another kiss. Out of the corner of her eyes she could see him shut the door with his foot, and she dragged him down the short hallway to her bedroom, grabbing at his pants as they walked. Not able to move the button or the zipper on his jeans, she shrugged off her jacket, unbuttoned her shirt, and let it fall to the floor.

Atlas raked off his shirt and threw it aside as they both stumbled toward her room, and then fell back against her bed. With two swift kicks, her boots went flying, and then she started working on her jeans. Her thumbs fumbled with the button, and he swiped her hands away and undid her pants, and then worked them down her legs and onto the floor.

"Are you sure you are okay with this? I don't want you to think I'm taking advantage of you."

"I am very sure that I want this." Siobhan smoothed her hands over his abs and upward over his shoulders, and then down his biceps.

Atlas shivered, took her wrists in one hand, and placed them above her head. Then he leaned over her body. Taking one of her lace-covered nipples in his mouth, he suckled her breast. His bright blue eyes had taken on a darker color as he looked at her. Releasing her hands, he unclasped the front of her bra. The lace bra sprung free, and her large breasts sprang out as if begging for him to take them. He took her left breast into his mouth.

Her hips bucked off the bed. While he worked at her breast, his hands removed his pants and he threw them over the end of the bed. Looking down the length of his body, she could see that he'd gone commando. His penis had sprung free and was a long thick rod. Her hands moved from his arms and down to his cock, and she grasped and started to stroke up and down.

Atlas's head lolled forward, and his biceps tensed. Suddenly, he looked up and grabbed her panties and yanked them down her leg and tossed them aside. He pulled at her hips and rubbed his hands around the innermost part of her thighs, just touching the hair around her pulsing core. His stroking came closer and closer to her center. He moved his index finger to the tip of the bud and stroked it while he moved his other hand to enter her channel.

Her legs quivered with the anticipation building inside her. As his finger began to enter and her hips jerked up, his finger slid into her body. A deep moan left her lips, and her head fell back on to the bed.

With quick strokes, he continued to rub her bud as he moved his fingers in and out of her passage. She felt her insides begin to coil as his strokes got faster and faster, and then it felt as if the world had fallen away as she came apart. Suddenly, he pulled his hands from her legs and moved off the bed.

"Is everything ok?" she gasped.

"Yes, just grabbing a condom. I'll be right back."

Then he was back over her again, his hands rubbing down her arms and over her stomach then down her thighs again. Siobhan felt her legs relax, but when he touched her pussy again, her hips bucked.

"Are you ready?" he rasped.

"Oh, yes." A moan escaped her throat. She felt his thickness as he pushed into her.

"Ohhh." Another moan came, this one from him. "You feel so good."

"So do you." Meeting him stroke for stroke, desire coiled inside her, winding tighter and tighter. Following a flurry of short, hard thrusts, she felt pleasure cascade over her and sagged back on the bed.

Just as she fell back, Atlas gave a shout and collapsed over her. He breathed deeply, twice, then rolled to his side, taking her with him. Both panted heavily. Then as their breaths slowed, they closed their eyes.

Siobhan slept through the night. When her alarm rang, she rolled over onto a crisp white pillow and saw a white folded note on her night stand.

It read:

I enjoyed spending time with you. Call me when you get a break from surgery.

No phone number was added but a unit number was listed, and it was signed J.B. Wayne "Atlas".

CHAPTER 1

Six years later....

"Dr. Monahan, room three is a broken toe, and room two looks like an asthma attack. Room two is currently getting a breathing treatment."

"Thank you, Nurse Shelly. Can you wrap up this patient's arm, and I'll look in on room two?"

"Will do, Doc."

Siobhan loved working in the emergency room because the hours flew by until the time she got to go home to her beautiful little girl.

That little girl's name was Mable, and Mable was her entire life.

They lived in a perfect little subdivision on the

outskirts of Seattle with her grandfather. Her grandfather was a Vietnam Veteran, who was very protective of his family. He helped her with the day to day of raising a little girl while she supported them by working.

"Hey Doc, looks like a VIP just walked in. I'll put them in room four."

"Thanks, I'll be right there." Finishing up the chart she was looking at, she walked over to the glass door of room 4. Outside the room stood two very large men wearing black military grade uniforms and Kevlar. Both stood with their feet shoulder width apart, and they stopped her when she tried to enter to room, blocking her way.

She tilted her chin while raising both brows. Men in uniform did not intimidate her. "I'm Dr. Monahan, and I am here to see the patient in this room."

The man nearest her turned away and touched the ear piece he wore in his right ear. From what she could hear of this muffled voice, he spoke German. Each man had buzzed short hair but the nearest one to her had lighter, almost blonde hair, and the one on the left had black cropped hair.

Blondie turned to her, nodded his head, and opened the door to the room. Siobhan walked into the room like she normally did, but this time, there were more men in black military gear and cropped hair surrounding the bed. Blood covered the suit of the man lying in the bed. His chest was moving very shallowly. A woman wearing a red tracksuit stood over him. She had long auburn hair and was speaking German rapidly to the man in the suit. When one of the guards bent to whisper to her, she straightened and glanced at Siobhan.

The Lady in Red spoke in English, "So you are the doctor we've been waiting for?"

"Yes, what's happened to him?"

She waved a hand toward the unconscious man. "He was in accident." In German, she said to the guard, "Stupid American doctor. Does she not know her own job?"

Siobhan felt like she had been mentally slapped with that comment, and it brought her back to this moment. Moving into action, she stepped over to the man in the suit and put her stethoscope into her ears and listened to his heartbeat. It was thready and indicated a possible heart issue, and she realized that she would need some help in here if she was going to save this man.

Just as she was about to shout for a nurse, she heard the guard say in German to the Lady in Red, "The package is delivered and in the General's hands. We need to patch up the captain and get back to the meeting point."

The Lady in Red turned to the guard, "You will do as you are told. We will have time to take out who we have been tasked to." They both looked at her, and she turned away to call for a nurse.

In German, she said to them, "I need for all of you to step back and let my team inside to help me so we can help your Captain." She hadn't spent most of her Army career in Germany without learning the language. Watching their widening eyes, gave her great satisfaction. Because she was female, too often, people underestimated her abilities and intelligence.

Walking over to the door, she shouted for nurses, and a tech to come draw blood. They all swarmed into the room, moving in unison, working on the man with the suit on the bed. Once they stabilized the patient, Siobhan moved to leave the room to check on her next patient. Just as she walked to the door, the Lady in Red stepped next to her.

She grabbed her arm, and in German, said, "Don't go far tonight. We have much to talk about." The woman released her arm and stepped away.

Siobhan knew this was not a good thing, and her military instincts came to the forefront in her head. After walking away from the room, she stopped to speak to the nurse at the desk. "I'm going to step away and make a call."

"All right, Doc."

She rushed down the hall and into the doctors' breakroom, and was relieved to find it empty. She needed privacy. From the side pocket of her white coat she pulled out her cellphone and dialed her grandfather. He'd know what to do.

"What's up, my sweet girl?" he answered.

"Grandad, I just helped some people here at work, and I think I might be in trouble."

"How so?" he asked.

She explained the situation and the woman in red's command.

Her grandfather paused and then said, "It pays to be cautious. As soon as you leave work, I want you to meet me and Mable at the bunker. You remember where it is?"

"Of course. I'll meet you there in an hour, and I'll call a friend of mine from my military days."

With her finger, she swiped to hang up her phone then searched her contacts for Hank Patterson, a friend she'd met while still a surgeon in the Army. Now, he ran a business called the Brotherhood Protectors, a group of men and women who helped others. They had all served in the military, and then were recruited by Hank.

"Hank, here," he answered on the first ring.

She sighed with relief. "Hey, it's Siobhan…Dr. Siobhan Monahan. Do you remember me?"

"Of course, I remember you. You saved many of my buddies' lives. What can I do for you, Doc?"

"I am pretty sure I got myself into some trouble here, and I could really use some of your expertise and help right now."

"What kind of trouble?"

"I work in an emergency room in a suburb of Seattle, and I just helped a patient that I think is possibly a part of a mercenary group or something of that sort. They were speaking German and said something about a package being delivered and picked up, and then meeting up with 'The General'. They referred to the man I was working on as the Captain, and there was a strange woman who seemed to be their leader. The guard were all dressed in military-grade black gear with Kevlar. They were talking about a package and taking someone out."

"Do you have somewhere safe you can go until we can get to you?" Hank asked.

"My grandfather has a bunker in the woods

about an hour from Seattle. He'll meet me there with my daughter. I can text you the coordinates."

"Ok, I will send a couple of my specialists out there to you. It may be a few hours before they get there but don't talk to anyone else. The lead's code name is Atlas. We'll track you through your phone, but no one else will be able to tag on once we get a lock on you. Also, I'll have my computer analyst start looking into any German militant or mercenary groups in your area, so we know who we're dealing with."

"Thank you, Hank. Will do" She hung up the phone, changed her clothes and grabbed her purse from her wall locker.

Rushing out of the locker room and flagged down her shift manager.

"Hey Jill, sorry I have an emergency at home."

"No Worries Siobhan, your shift is almost over, let me know if you need anything."

"Ok thanks will do."

She headed the back way out of the building to the employee parking garage. Her grandfather always drove his old Chevy truck but made sure it was always in good repair and running beautifully. They'd agreed that she should have the latest model vehicle since she was a doctor and took Mable to her ballet classes when she wasn't working. Her grandfather took Mable to most of her practices, but didn't want to give up his truck, and traded vehicles when needed. She had a nice big black 4Runner with all the latest gadgets.

As she walked up to her car, she noticed a black SUV parked to the side of the parking lot. At first, she thought nothing of it, but then the hairs on the back of her neck came to attention, and all those years of being in the military kicked in. Looking around the parking lot, she did a quick sweep of her surroundings and picked up her pace, not quite at a run, but a speed walk. She kept her gaze focused ahead so as not to draw attention.

The last few steps seemed to take an eternity, but she reached her vehicle and jumped in. With a push to the start button, she revved the engine and put her car into gear. With a few quick turns in the parking lot, she was on the main road headed to the bunker.

Watching her rearview mirror, she saw the black SUV swing onto the road behind her. So much for getting this done quickly.

ATLAS FELT a dread wash over him when he heard

Hank call for him. After having worked for Hank for several years now, he normally was sent out with a group of guys, but this would be his first mission as lead, and with a newbie no less. Since he always had a go bag, he grabbed it and headed out of the ranch house and the helicopter his boss kept on standby for special missions.

He nodded at Brotherhood Protector Wooten, codename "Soldier". He was new to their civilian group but had served in the military as spec ops for SEAL Team 6, just like Atlas, and always looked as if he was still active duty. Hair high and tight, clothes pressed with a crease, and spit-shined boots.

The helicopter they boarded for the flight to Seattle was no ordinary civilian helo. It had been upgraded and was large, like the ones he'd flown while in the military. He hadn't flown in a helo since that fateful day when he'd been injured. Those injuries had resulted in his being medically discharged.

Shaking his head, he pushed those memories aside. He needed his head on straight so that he could go through the current scenario and decide what needed to be done. Of course, his first priority was getting to the woman and her child, and make sure they were safe. Next, they'd need to figure out who the people who threatened her were and what they wanted. Once they were neutralized, Atlas was going to have a long conversation with Dr. Siobhan Monahan. The women he'd fallen for at first glance. For years, he'd regretted the fact he'd left her after their one and only meeting, and hadn't heard from her, until now.

Before Atlas realized it, the helicopter was descending, and they were touching down. He grabbed his pack and jumped out, making sure that his six-foot-one frame was slightly hunched over so as not to be decapitated by the blades circling over-head. Soldier ran alongside him with his own go bag in hand. Their boots pounded on the pavement as the helo took off in the starless night sky.

"So, what's the plan, Atlas?" Soldier asked.

As they ran to the other side of the helicopter pad atop a bank building to head down the stairs, he didn't miss a beat, talking loudly over his shoulder, "First things first, we need to find Dr. Monahan, and get to her daughter and grandfather in this so-called bunker. Then we need to decide what needs to be done before we go after these guys."

Just outside of the building they exited, a driver stood by to deliver the vehicle they'd be using while they were protecting Siobhan and her family. It was early morning now but still dark out. Very few cars could be seen driving the streets in the area where they'd landed.

Both men stowed their bags in the trunk of the black SUV and jumped into the front of the vehicle, Atlas driving and Soldier riding shot-gun. His teammate pulled out his phone and opened to the GPS app, which was synced to Siobhan's phone so that they could track her movements and get to her.

Soldier turned toward Atlas and directed him to turn left. "I think she's in trouble. It looks like she is taking more than a normal amount of turns, like she's trying to lose someone. We better hurry."

Atlas felt a chill go down his spine and let it flow out of his body as he turned the SUV in the direction Soldier said to turn, picking up speed as he straightened up on the road.

"We're close now, but it looks like her vehicle has picked up speed. If you turn right here, we'll come up next to her."

Following the directions, Atlas swung the vehicle out on the road, just as a smaller SUV that matched the description in the file of one of Siobhan's vehicles sped by them with a large black SUV close behind it. Not wasting any time, Atlas sped down the road behind the dark vehicle and pulled up next to it on the two-lane street and moved his vehicle to clip the side of its door. Just then the other vehicle's windows cracked open and a gun poked out.

"Gun!" Atlas bit out as he moved Soldier out of the way.

He slammed his foot on the gas and sped past as the back window of their SUV shattered under the gunfire. He zagged in front of the dark SUV and pressed the brakes. The SUV swerved to avoid crashing into them and ran into a street sign. Atlas picked up speed to try to catch up to the smaller vehicle that had passed them earlier. As they came up close to the vehicle that the GPS indicated was Siobhan's, it sped up again. Atlas flashed his lights at her and the driver slowed down slightly, he pulled up next to her and rolled down his window and motioned for her to do the same. He pulled out his cellphone and called the number that Hank had given him for Siobhan. She answered the phone, "Hank?"

"No, it's Atlas, remember he said he would be sending us to help you. Pull over in the alleyway up ahead."

"Okay," the other vehicle's window came down, and he could see reddish blond hair swept up in a pony tail and a pale face that shined like a beacon from the dark interior. He motioned for her to pull over into an alley up ahead.

They followed behind her, and as he stopped his vehicle and exited, she jumped out of her car and leaned her back up against it. With quick strides, he was next to her and she leaned toward him, almost falling over. Putting his arms around her waist, he kept her on her feet. Her breaths came hard and fast.

"Oh, am I glad to see you guys, Atlas," she panted. "I can't believe you're here."

Her breathing was slowing down, and his grip on her waist loosened. "What happened when you left the hospital? I thought you would be at the bunker by now?"

"When I left the hospital, there was an SUV following me. I was able to lose them for a short time and went to my house to make sure my family made it out safely. There, I grabbed a few supplies. Once I left, they found me again, and I've been trying to lose them ever since."

"We need to get you to the bunker and your family, and then we can make a plan for what we're going to do next."

Atlas turned to Soldier, who had come up beside them while they were talking.

"Boss, we better leave her vehicle, just in case they've somehow planted a tracker on it."

"Good thinking, Soldier."

He glanced down at Siobhan. "Grab your stuff, and we'll go in our vehicle."

She looked around and grimaced. "All right, if you think it would be the best thing, but can we move my car to a safer location?"

"We better leave it here for now. Hank can have a tow company come pick it up shortly to store it until we come get it."

She nodded. "That sounds good to me. Let me just grab my stuff."

"Here let me help you with that," he said, tossing the keys to Soldier. "Start our vehicle, while I help Dr. Monahan. Call in an anonymous tip to the cops for our friends back there."

"Roger"

"Atlas, you guys can call me Siobhan," she said and then turned her face away, but not before he saw a blush come over her pretty face.

Holding her in his arms had felt good, as if they'd been together always. He'd dreamed about her for years especially after his accident.

When she bent over to get the bags out of the back seat of her small SUV, he noticed how her jeans stretched over her firm, round bottom. With great effort, he turned to see what she was doing and reached past her to grab for one of the two bags she was trying to haul out.

"Let me get that for you."

"Thanks," she said, her gaze sliding away. "I'm ready when you guys are."

He put her bags in the trunk and made sure she was ok in the backseat before climbing into the driver's seat. "Where to, Siobhan?"

"Just head straight on this road. It leads to the old highway that will take us out to the woods where the bunker is."

Once on the road again, Siobhan sat silently in the backseat. Atlas kept looking at her in the rearview mirror, seeing her as he remembered.

After a while, she said in a soft voice, "We're almost there. Turn down that dirt road just ahead on the right."

Visibility was horrible because of the near-pitch darkness caused by the thick canopy of trees overhead, so he had to slow down to see the small dirt road.

"You'll follow this road for a few minutes. I'll tell you when to stop. We'll have to walk a short distance into the wood."

They drove a few more minutes through the down the road past more trees.

"Pull over here."

He did as she directed and parked his vehicle. Then he walked toward the trunk to get their bags.

"I can take that," Siobhan said. Her hand came over his to stop him from grabbing the second of her two bags.

When their hands touched, he felt it deep down, and his cock sprang to life. Clearing his throat, he said, "After you."

They all pulled out flashlights from their bags.

Siobhan began to turn away and said, "Follow me." She seemed to hesitate just as he heard a branch break behind them. He grabbed Siobhan and motioned for Soldier to take cover. Just then a rifle shot rang out somewhere in the woods. Atlas pulled Siobhan to his body and they fell behind a large bolder to their right.

He leaned over to pull his handgun from his back holster, then whispered to Siobhan, "Stay down."

CHAPTER 2

Siobhan's heart beat so rapidly she felt it like it would push right out of her chest. Hunkering down behind the rock, she couldn't see what was happening in the forest. Atlas and Soldier each had a fire arm out with what looked like night vision scopes on them and were darting glances around boulders to see where the shots were coming from. From where they had taken shelter from the gunfire, she could just make out the entrance to the cave where her grandfather had installed an underground shelter. The headlights from their SUV lit the side of the cave, even though it was about 25 yards away in the woods, there was also a slight path through the trees, and she knew that the entrance was not easily seen if you didn't know what you were looking at.

Little Mable and her grandfather would be safe in there, but how she could get to them without being noticed?

Atlas hunkered down again.

"We are really close to the entrance," she whispered. "What's our next move?"

He motioned to Soldier with hand signals then looked back at her. "We're going to create a distraction so you can get to the shelter, and then will come back for you guys once the area's clear of the danger."

"If the others see where I go, they'll know where to look."

"Don't worry. We have you covered' once your clear run like the hellhounds of Hades are on your heels, got it?"

"Okay." Her hair had come loose from her ponytail holder and was swinging around her shoulders; she shoved it behind her, as she nodded her head in agreement.

"Go now," he said so suddenly that it took her a few seconds to realize what he'd said.

"Go!"

With a quick jump into the air, she sprang from behind the cold rock and sprinted across the forest to the cave, her flash light clutched in her hand. All she could think of was getting to the shelter and to her daughter. As she neared, she slowed. Since the ceiling was fairly low, she bent at the waist, enough to enter the cave, and then continued along the path to the right. The entrance was camouflaged by an old mining door. Siobhan kicked the old crate that had been bolted to the door in the ground, revealing the keypad to the shelter. Once she entered the code, a beep sounded, and the pressurized door popped open.

Siobhan opened the door wider and went down the stairs inside the bunker, the door automatically closing behind her. She held out her hands to trail them along the walls so that she could go down the steps in the darkness. A light could be seen at the end of the little stairwell. Everything in the entrance was metal, and her footsteps rang out in the silence. As she stepped down onto the main level, she came up short, seeing her grandfather standing there holding a rifle, her little girl peeking from behind him with her blanket and a doll in her arms.

Recognizing her, her grandfather let out a deep breath and put down the weapon. With steady steps, he moved forward and grabbed her into a big bear hug. "Girlie, you just about scared me off this earth."

"Sorry, Pop," she said, slightly out of breath. "It's been a day."

"I can see that. Why don't you sit down in the lounge? I'll make you a cup of tea, and you can tell me all about it."

"First let me see my little one," she said, forcing a smile on her face as she walked over to the precious little girl with the strawberry-blonde hair and clear blue eyes.

"How are you, my little strawberry?" she said and swooped up her little girl.

With a little hoot and a giggle, her daughter cuddled into her arms.

"Pop-Pop picked me up from school early, Momma."

She smiled down at her daughter. "He did, did he?"

"Yeah, and then we drove all the way here, and then we played games and ate snacks and watched movies. There are some old movies here, Momma."

Siobhan gave a short laugh. "Yes, there are. We may need to update them one of these days," she said, grinning over at her granddad.

"That we should," he said.

"All right, little priss," Siobhan said, giving her a

final hug. "Why don't you go play with Dolly while I talk to Pop-Pop?"

"Okay," she said, and bounded off to some toys that were scattered in the lounge area.

When Siobhan turned from her daughter playing on the floor, a hot mug of tea was handed to her by her grandfather.

In his stern military voice, low enough the little girl couldn't hear, he said, "Story, now."

She nodded. "So, you remember what I told you when I was at the hospital, right?"

"Yes." He motioned her to take a seat at the small table at the end of the kitchenette.

"Well, I called Hank, an old friend of mine from my military days. He has his own security company. I asked him to send some help." Just then a banging sound echoed through the underground area, coming from the entrance. She glanced up the hallway and then at her grandfather, who was already grabbing the rifle. He handed her a tablet, opened to the app that displayed video feed from the camera at the door.

"If you had this the whole time, why did you almost shoot me earlier with the rifle?" she muttered.

"Someone could have been behind you. First

signal from you, and I would have blasted his head off," he said with a big grin.

"All right, cowboy, let's see who it is."

On the screen stood Soldier and under his arm was a very bloody looking Atlas.

ATLAS FELT his vision coming and going as he leaned against Soldier who stood in front of a strange looking door in the cave Siobhan had disappeared inside.

As she ran from them, Atlas had stood up from the rock they'd used as cover. He'd laid down a blanket of bullets to distract their attackers, so that she could get to the bunker. For several minutes more, he and Soldier continued returning fire, not allowing Siobhan's attackers anywhere near the cave. Then he'd noticed a car peeling out and racing away. With a heavy sigh, Atlas had scanned the forest to make sure no one else would follow them but hadn't seen anyone. Silence fell over the clearing. Soldier moved next to him and hunkered down. Atlas slid his back down the boulder and sat.

"Looks like they left. Wonder why?" Soldier said, and then glanced over at the cave hidden in the forest.

"Probably to report to their higherups and to bring in reinforcements. We need to get moving."

"Well, let's go," Soldier said, pushing away from the rock, still scanning the area. He pulled out a flash light and pointed it toward the cave. Before making their way to the cave they grabbed the bags from the vehicle.

Following behind Soldier, Atlas moved at a jog. They ran side by side for the short distance, with their flashlights bouncing along the trail. The cave entrance came up fast. Suddenly Atlas felt a sharp pain in his head, and he staggered then bent over from the pain.

Soldier turned and leaned over to check on Atlas. "Atlas, are you okay, man?"

Atlas grimaced. "Yeah, I'm an idiot. I was watching the flashlight following the ground and didn't realize that the cave entrance dipped down right there. Good thing I have a hard head," he said, reaching up to touch his scalp and finding moisture there.

From his right side, Soldier chuckled as he dragged Atlas's arm over his shoulder. "Sorry to tell you this man, but you're bleeding like a stuck pig."

"Yeah, having trouble seeing 'cause blood's in my eyes."

"Come on. It can't be that far. I can see where her feet scuffed the dirt, so it shouldn't be that hard to follow her steps."

"Sounds good to me. On to the doctor."

They stumbled further into the cave and followed the footprints until they stopped at a strange door. Soldier hesitated, then he reached forward and banged on what appeared to be an old mine door. Atlas stumbled forward slightly, and Soldier had to move his feet so he wouldn't fall over.

"I think I might have hit my head harder than I thought," Atlas mumbled.

"Yup, I agree with you."

Suddenly, the ground beneath them moved, and Soldier pulled him back so that they wouldn't fall into an opening.

Siobhan's voice came from below, "Pops, it's the men who helped me get here. The ones Hank sent. They're good to go."

Atlas started to move forward, and Soldier struggled to get down the steps into the bunker while trying to keep Atlas propped up as he walked down. Through his blurred vision, he could see Siobhan rush up to meet them and take Atlas's other arm to help him down the rest of the way.

"Did you get shot? Let me look at you," she said

as she led him over to the lounge chair in the little living area.

He collapsed onto the chair. An older man holding a rifle in one hand leaned over and gave him a towel. Grasping the towel, he wiped at his face to get the blood out of his eyes.

"Thank you, sir," he said, and then turned to Siobhan. "I hit my head when we entered the cave. It's just a head wound."

"Oh, my goodness, glad to hear it," she said as she leaned over with a penlight to flash it into his eyes. "You may have a mild concussion, but without an MRI, I can't be sure. We'll have to watch you for about 24 hours."

She probed around his injury.

"Ouch, that hurts."

"Are you okay m-mister?" a little girl asked in a tiny voice.

He looked down at her and noticed she had long, curly red-blonde hair and crystal-blue eyes.

Siobhan turned to the little girl. "Mable why don't you go play with your dolls, while I fix this man?"

"Okay, Momma." She skipped off to the other side of the bunker.

"Is that your daughter?" Atlas asked.

"Yes." She didn't look him in the eyes as she examined his head. Her touch was gentle on his skin, but the pressure of her fingers on his wound caused some pain, and he flinched.

"Sorry," she said. "I think I'm going to have to put a couple of stitches in that so the bleeding will stop."

"How old is she?" Atlas wanted to know.

Siobhan didn't answer. She pulled a small kit out of her bag next to the chair on the floor and set out gauze and cleaning supplies. With the gauze, she cleaned his head, which hurt, but he was distracted from the pain as he waited to hear what she would say. The needle and thread flashed in front of his face, and he felt the first sting as it entered his flesh.

Gritting his teeth, he held still.

"Mable is just five," she said in a soft voice.

Atlas's world seemed to spin, not from the head wound or the pain from the stitches, but because he remembered the time, six years ago when he'd met this beautiful woman. The night when they'd had a one-night stand.

"Yes, Atlas," she whispered, glancing down into his eyes. "She's your daughter."

CHAPTER 3

SIOBHAN COULD FEEL the weight of the secret leave her body, but at the same time she felt uneasy with Atlas's gaze on her. His level stare caused an ache of regret, because, deep down, she knew what she'd done was wrong.

The night they'd spent at the bar so long ago in Germany, he'd told her the military was his entire life, and he couldn't see himself doing anything else.

Her dream had always been to move back to Washington state one day, and to have a family with a house and a white picket fence. When little Mable had come, her life changed a lot faster and sooner than she'd originally planned, and she'd had to reorganize her plans.

Getting out of the military and moving back

home had been her first step. Back to Seattle, where her family was from. Both of her parents had died in a car accident when she was in medical school, and the only family she had left was her grandfather.

He was a gruff old veteran but had opened his home to her while she'd been pregnant and had helped her through that time.

Once she'd recovered from giving birth to Mable, he'd taken over watching and caring for her daughter while Siobhan had gone back to work at a local hospital in its ER.

Grandpa had loved looking after the little girl and took her to pre-school and her practices for soccer and dance. Mable was a very active little girl, and they had both decided that the more activities she could be involved in, the better. Even at five years old, she had an abundance of energy that her pediatrician was surprised by.

Her daughter sidled up beside her and leaned against her leg. "Momma, is the man going to be okay?"

"Yes, my sweet, he was just surprised and hit his head."

"Oh, okay, will you play dollies with me?"

She smoothed her hand over her daughter's curly hair. "It's your bedtime. Let's get you cleaned up and in your bed." They would be safe in the bunker, because of how well fortified her grandfather had constructed the space. The later alterations they had made to it, they'd done together. They even had electricity and running water.

"Awww… I want to stay up and play," Mable said.

She stroked her daughter's soft curls. "Sorry, we've had an eventful day, and you need to go to bed so you can be rested for tomorrow."

The little girl pushed out her lower lip, and her shoulders slumped.

"Come on, Mable," Siobhan said. "Don't pout. I'll read you a story, and then tuck you in. Say goodnight to the nice men, and Pops, too."

She watched as her little one turned to the two men and said goodnight.

Atlas seemed to want to do something, but then his body went rigid, and he smiled with his lips and not his eyes. "Goodnight, princess," he said to her.

"Goodnight, mister."

"You can call me Atlas, if you want…"

"Okay."

Then she bounded over to her grandfather.

The old man wrapped his arms around her in a big bear hung and swung her in the air.

"All right, Grandad," Siobhan said. "You'll get her all wound up again."

She smiled over at him, and he looked over at her while still holding the little girl up.

His eyes seemed to sparkle. Then he lowered Mable to the floor, patted her head and turned her toward her bunk. "Off you go, little one."

Over the years since she'd moved back, they'd set up the space so that Mable would feel at home. They'd added amenities and new technology so they would feel safe, too. Mable had thought of their visits to the bunker as camping and loved to come. Siobhan had gone along with her grandfather's paranoia from the Cold War era. She knew it made him feel comfortable to know they would always have somewhere safe to go.

She moved over to the little bunk covered in a pink comforter with little characters printed on it, and the dolls and bears strewn all over it. With a swift swipe of her arm, she pushed the toys into the basket that had been pulled out from under the bunk and deposited them back into their home. With her foot, she pushed the short basket under the bed and pulled down the covers so that her daughter could climb into bed. Mable hopped onto the mattress, shoved her feet under the covers, and scooted down so that she could rest her strawberry-blonde head on the pillow. Her daughter's and her beds were situated at the end of the room, and her grandfather had a bed set up at the end of the living area, near the entrance. He had done that on purpose so that he could "stand guard".

After reading Mable a story, Siobhan gave her child a smile. "Goodnight, precious."

Mable reached up and pulled Siobhan's head down for a loud smacking kiss on her cheek. "Love you, Momma."

Siobhan leaned over and kissed her daughter's forehead. "Love you, too."

Mable rolled onto her side, facing the wall. The little girl always fell asleep as soon as her head hit the pillow.

Siobhan stood then turned back to head over to the lounge area, trying not to look at Atlas.

"Alright, boys," her grandfather said, "the couch and the lounge chairs all fold out into beds. There are linens, blankets and pillows in the chest in the middle of the sitting area."

Atlas nodded. "Thank you, sir, we'll set up for the night."

Since the guys were getting situated, she decided to head over to her bed and get settled in for the night. They came here so often; she had a small amount of clothing and the essentials that she would need. She slid the bin out from beneath her bed and pulled out a toothbrush and toothpaste. After gathering her toiletries, she headed over to the full bathroom they had installed.

Atlas met her on her way across the room. "We need to talk."

Siobhan sighed. "Can it wait until tomorrow? I'm really tired."

He drew a deep breath. "Yeah, but no more running away."

She met his gaze with a steady one of her own. "I never ran away from this." She walked into the bathroom and closed the door in his face.

WHY WAS she hiding from him after dropping the proverbial bomb on him? He had so many questions to ask her about his daughter. Deciding that he would sleep on it after Siobhan's blunt refusal to talk tonight, Atlas walked over to the pull-out couch where Soldier and Pat, Siobhan's grandfather, where discussing the different countries they had traveled to.

"You still prefer a pizza from America and not from Italy?" Soldier said, his eyebrows rising.

"Son, sometimes, home is best, no matter how good it is elsewhere."

"Very true." Solider nodded. "There's no place like home."

Atlas piped in at that moment, "Chicago has the best pizza anywhere."

"I don't know. I'd say New York has the best." Soldier grabbed a blanket out of the chest and tossed a pillow at Atlas.

A little giggle could be heard from the other side of the room.

Atlas turned his head toward the little bed where his daughter was laying. She had rolled over to look at them while they set up the beds and had seen Soldier tossing the pillow.

Pat turned to his great-granddaughter and motioned for her to come over to them. She jumped out of the bed, and like a gazelle, she bounded across the floor and into his arms. Atlas felt a pang of loss in his chest. In that moment, he realized how much he had missed by not knowing his daughter.

"Little miss, do you want me to read you another story before you go to sleep?"

"Uh huh," she nodded her head in agreement.

"Go grab a book from your bookshelf and bring it back."

As before, Atlas watched his daughter bound across the room to a little shelf filled with books and toys at the end of her bed. Once she got her book, she hurried back to her grandfather's lap. Soldier was putting a sheet on the pull-out bed, and Atlas turned to get the blankets. He could hear Pat tell the story to the little girl with animated voices, and the little girl, giggled along with him. Atlas finished putting the blankets on the beds, and Soldier grabbed the pillows from the lounge chair to put on bed as well. At that moment, the door to the bathroom opened, and Siobhan walked out. Somehow, Pat had set up a fully functioning shower, and Siobhan's hair was wet. Atlas was mesmerized by her beauty, and her movements were so graceful.

She ignored his gaze and looked over to their daughter. "Come on, Mable. It's bedtime."

"Ahhh, Momma," Mable cried, "the story is almost over."

"We can finish it tomorrow, little one," Pat said. "You should listen to your mom."

Mable got up slowly and dragged her feet toward the bed. Her head hung down, and her blonde hair swung in her face.

Atlas had to fight a smile at the contrast to her earlier speed; she almost looked like a miniature zombie.

Siobhan helped Mable into bed again. Then she dried her hair and settled in her own bed while the guys talked in hushed tones.

Pat turned out the lights in the living area, but there was a nightlight shining by the bed where Mable slept.

Atlas struggled to fall asleep with his thoughts all over the place, thinking about Mable and Siobhan. He finally felt enough at ease that he dozed off. His dreams always seemed to go back to the day he was injured.

They had been dropped into an area near a remote village in the Middle East. The desert was cooling since the sun was no longer out, and the night air carried the scent of cooking spices. His men had been told there was a female informant living in a compound with her family, and only 3-4 men inside whom they could easily take out. When they got to the compound, all was quiet.

Atlas was always on guard, but the night before, he'd been thinking about the beautiful doctor and the way the bar's lights had shone on her strawberry-blonde hair. Just ahead of him was a little girl laying on a pallet inside the first main room. The TV was on, and she had fallen asleep watching it. The little girl blinked her eyes open and looked up at them. Just then, he heard a whooshing sound, and his buddy fell over. Then another whoosh sounded, and Atlas felt pain in his knee and a warm wet sensation oozing down his leg. He tried to hold in his shout of pain, but he grunted when his leg gave out. Quickly, he spoke into his mic in low tones, warning the rest of his unit what had happened.

Atlas felt a tiny hand on his arm, and he jerked awake. He looked up into blue eyes that reflected the glow from the nightlight. Those eyes that were like his had concern in them.

In a small whisper, the little angel asked, "Are you okay, mister?"

Taking a deep breath, he sat up slightly and nodded at the little girl.

"Your eyes look like mine," she said, tilting her head.

"Yes, they do. We both have blue eyes."

She tilted her head. "My mom's eyes are green."

"You're correct," he said, his voice a little rough. "Shouldn't you be in bed?"

"I heard you talking in your sleep, and it sounded like you were sad."

"Oh, well I have bad dreams, sometimes," he said as he stood up. He motioned for the girl to follow him toward her bed.

"I have bad dreams, too. There are dragons and dinosaurs in my dreams. What are your dreams about?"

Atlas didn't want to think any more about his dreams, but he also didn't want to disappoint her. "Well, my dreams don't have dinosaurs or dragons in them."

They had reached her bed by this time. He glanced over at Siobhan and could see that she was cocooned in her blankets with her back to them. Atlas helped the little girl get back in her bed and knelt next to her on the floor. His knee felt stiff, but he could be closer to her this way.

"Try thinking about rainbows and bunnies when you're trying to go to sleep, and I bet you'll dream about them, too."

"I love rainbows and bunnies," she said in a hushed, excited voice.

Atlas chuckled under his breath then reached over and pushed her hair gently out of her face before tucking her blanket around her shoulders. "Go to sleep, sweet girl, and I'll think about bunnies and rainbows, too."

"Okay," she said and settled into her pillow. When her eyes closed, she seemed to fall asleep, instantly.

Atlas went back to his sleeping area and found a comfortable spot. This time when he went to sleep, he dreamed about a little girl with blue eyes and blonde hair, playing with bunnies while a rainbow arched in the sky over them. A woman with straw-berry-blonde hair and green eyes smiled up at him as they held hands.

CHAPTER 4

SIOBHAN WOKE to the smell of bacon. It seemed to settle into her nostrils and beckon for her to get out of bed. Sitting up, it took her a minute to realize where she was and what had happened the day before. After getting up several times during the night to check on Atlas she was still groggy. Atlas, Soldier and her grandfather were talking to Mable and telling her a story. From what she could hear, the story was not completely appropriate for little ears, but her daughter was giggling.

Siobhan threw off the covers and swung her legs over the edge of the mattress. Slipping her feet into the slippers on the floor, she stood and walked over to the group to see what they were fixing for breakfast.

Atlas turned to face her as she approached. "Breakfast is almost done if you want to get the table ready…"

"Come on, Mable," she said, holding out her hand. "Let's set the table."

"Ok, Momma." The little girl bounded around the table, wrapped her arms around her mother's hips, and then skipped back to her grandfather to get the silverware he was carrying.

"Walk slowly, little one, and be careful," her grandfather said.

"Okay, Pop," Mable sang.

Soldier brought the plates. The three of them set the table while Atlas continued telling stories of misadventures his fellow soldiers had had while he served and set out the plates of food so that they could dish it out Thanksgiving style. The meal was delicious.

As they were finishing up breakfast, Mable turned to Atlas. "You're funny."

"Thank you, little lady." Atlas smiled at the little girl with a twinkle in his eye.

With Mable and Atlas sitting next to each other and interacting, Siobhan could see that her daughter definitely looked like her daddy. Everyone stood and moved to carry their dishes back to the kitchenette.

She turned to get up and felt a warm, solid hand on her shoulder. With a sharp look over her shoulder, she could see Atlas looking down at her.

His eyes a crystal blue. "Stay here and finish up your meal. We can clean up."

"No, I'm finished," she said. "You cooked. The least I can do is help clean up."

Atlas turned to Soldier, "Hey, man, can you clear the table? Siobhan and I will clean and dry the dishes."

He put his hand out toward her and helped her out of the chair. Together, they walked over to the sink. She filled it with soapy hot water, and he picked up the drying towel. She washed the dishes while he dried them.

"I was thinking that we should go find out if Hank has heard anything, and then make a plan of how to deal with the situation you have yourself in."

"I want to go with you," she said under her breath.

He put his hands on her shoulders and turned her toward him. She noted the muscles rippling in his arms and could feel his warm breath on her cheek.

"That's not a good idea. You need to stay here with Mable and your grandfather until we can figure out how to handle the problem. I need you to be safe."

"If you haven't forgotten, I know what most of the main players in this little game look like. You need me to identify them, just as much as I need you guys to keep me safe."

Frowning, Atlas nodded. "First, we need to see what intel Hank has gotten for us."

Siobhan got Mable dressed and playing with her toys. Her grandfather was reading a book in the sitting area.

Atlas and Soldier left the bunker to call Hank and see what intel they'd gathered since this had all started. It seemed like a week had passed, but it was barely 24 hours later. Her thoughts started to drift into a daydream of Atlas and Mable sitting at a little child's play table. Then another of the three of them running through a meadow with a dog romping around them.

A knock sounded at the bunker door and startled her out of the thoughts.

Pop looked at the screen showing the front door then pushed some buttons to let the guys back in.

Siobhan headed over to where they gathered with her grandfather.

"Hank and his IT guy found out that the group

you came across is delivering a package, and it has something to do with the Vice President's speech that's happening this afternoon. The local university is doing an outdoor event for up-and-coming gradu-ates, and they think the Vice President will be the target of an assassination attempt."

Siobhan's heart skipped several beats. "What are we waiting for? We need to head down there. It's only a few hours away."

"We will. First, I need to get your grandfather and Mable settled with Soldier, and then we'll meet up with some of the other guys Hank sent last night to help after he got this intel. They also notified the police and Secret Service so they will be monitoring the situation as well. When we meet up with the men Hank sent, the police will be there to go over with what you heard."

"Oh, okay, wow." She smiled. "Hank doesn't waste any time, does he?"

Atlas nodded. "No, he doesn't."

Mable came over and tugged on the bottom of Siobhan's shirt. "What's happening, Momma?"

Siobhan squatted down to be on her level. "Sweetie, Atlas and I need to go take care of some business, and Soldier is going to stay here with you and Pop."

Her little brow furrowed. "But I want to come with you guys."

Siobhan shook her head and tucked a strand of hair behind her daughter's ear. "No sweetie, it's better if you stay here. I need you to take care of Pop, okay?"

In a quiet but whiny voice, she said, "Yes, Momma." The little girl dragged her feet as she walked over to her toys that were lying on the floor in her play area, near the beds.

Siobhan turned to Atlas. "Let me get a couple things, and then I'll be ready to go. And Atlas, I also need to check your stitches before we leave."

"Roger," he said as she walked away.

As Siobhan neared her daughter, Mable's little face turned up toward her and the sparkle of curiosity was there in her eyes.

Kneeling on the floor next to her daughter, Siobhan stroked her blonde hair, and then pulled her into her lap for a bear hug.

"Momma, you're crushing me," Mable said in a muffled voice.

"Sorry, sweetie. I just love you so much. You listen to Soldier and Pops and make sure to keep them out of trouble for me, okay?"

"Okay, love you, too." Then Mable turned to go back to her toys.

Atlas had found a spot to rest on the lounge chair.

Siobhan's bag was already sitting on the table in the makeshift living area. She sat next to him and took his head in her hands. With him so close, she noted his manly, earthy smell and could feel her nipples pebbling beneath her shirt. To distract herself, she went to work on his head, making sure that it was clean, and that the skin around the stitches wasn't infected.

"I guess you'll live," she said and smiled up at him.

The look he gave her could not have been any less than smoldering. A warm shiver went through her, and she looked away so that he couldn't see the blush that spread across her cheeks.

His warm hand cupped her chin and turned her face to look at him. "Thank you for doctoring me, Siobhan. I have the best surgeon in the world working on me."

"Well, I hate to tell you this, but I'm not a surgeon anymore. I'm an emergency room doctor now."

"Either way, I'm sure that you're the best."

Moving to put her supplies back into her bag, she then took the few things she had gathered and shoved them into a backpack she'd pulled out of the bin under her bed. "I'm ready when you are."

As she turned back to Atlas, she realized he had all his gear on and was waiting on her to go. When she'd been in the military, she'd been able to get ready quickly and had been out the door before most everyone else.

Her grandfather stepped up beside them, "I've got the little princess taken care of. You don't worry. Just make sure you stay safe."

"Will do, Pops," she said and gave him a hug.

Just as she started toward Atlas to head out, a flying ball of blonde collided with her, "Bye, Momma. I love you."

"Bye, Mable. Love you, too," she said, trying to not to cry and squeezing her closer to her face, so she could take in the little girl smell. On a sigh, she released her daughter and stepped away. She glanced at Soldier. "Please keep them safe," she said in a whisper.

He nodded in response and went to stand by her grandfather.

Back at Atlas's side, she moved with him to leave the bunker and to head to the vehicle.

. . .

ATLAS COULDN'T BELIEVE how fast everything was moving. He felt as though he was back in the military again. The big difference now was that he had a beautiful woman to protect and a daughter he wanted to get to know. Those were things that could not only distract him, but were also quickly becoming precious, and he didn't want to ruin his chance to get to know them both.

Over his shoulder, he could see Siobhan keeping pace with him as they made the short trek to the vehicle that had been hastily left last night. He kept an eye out to detect any potential ambushes, but Hank had called in a quick satellite image to them of the area, and there was no movement or vehicles around for miles. They would be safe in the isolated area to get to their vehicle, but he still wanted to be sure.

As they approached the car, he unlocked it with the key fob and motioned for Siobhan to get in the passenger side, while he moved to the driver side of the car. They threw their bags into the back seat of the vehicle. Once inside, he started up the engine and moved the car onto the path they'd come in on.

"What have you been up to the last few years?" she asked, her gaze looking forward.

He took a moment to answer her, trying to think

of how to answer her question and also to keep an eye on where he was driving through the trees. "I've been out of the military for the last five years and working with Hank basically since getting out."

"Oh, I thought you would've been a career military man."

"I was injured about a year after we met." His lips pressed together. "I was medically discharged from the military."

"Tell me what happened."

With a deep breath in, he started his story, "After we met, I went back to my unit. The next day back in Afghanistan. A few years went by it was on one of our numerous missions. We were on the path to an insurgent's compound. I was out in the open and on my way to the house that was in the center of the compound. I was distracted by a child in the house and didn't see the sniper in time. My buddy pushed me out of the way but not quickly enough that we both didn't get shot."

She nodded, her brow puckering.

Atlas cleared his throat. "Why didn't you call me?"

"I didn't really think you wanted a relationship." Her lips twisted. "I thought you were a military career man."

"What about when you got pregnant?" he asked.

She took a deep breath and then looked out the window of the car. They were on the highway now, and the trees passed by as if in a blur of green.

"By then, time had passed, and because I didn't want you distracted by a child, I made a command decision and called my grandfather. I got out of the military, settled in Seattle, and the rest is history."

His hands tightened on the steering wheel. "You should have let me know."

Siobhan nodded. "I know that now, but I was in a different place in my life and didn't know you. My parents had died, and the only family I had was my grandfather. I knew he would be there for us, so I decided to move to Seattle to raise my daughter and find a job."

They reached the facility where he was to meet the other guys, and he parked at the end of the line of their vehicles. He watched Kujo walking his dog, Six, in a little patch of grass by the road. Six had been with Kujo since they'd served in the military together. Each had sustained injuries while in the military and had been able to stay together when they were medically discharged.

Atlas motioned for Siobhan to follow him over to the man with his dog.

"Hey, It's good to see you guys, again," Atlas said, giving Kujo's hand a firm shake.

"Man, we need to stop meeting like this," Kujo said, grinning.

"I want to introduce you to Dr. Siobhan Monahan."

They all shook hands. Siobhan gave Kujo a tight smile. "It's very nice to meet you. Thank you for helping."

"It's our pleasure," Kujo said. "I wish it was under better circumstances."

Six led them into the building panting from his little walk in the heat and Kujo walked behind him. They came up to a work table where several of Hank's men were gathered as well as some plain-clothes police officers in windbreakers that said Police on the back of them. Everyone made introductions.

Kujo piped in, "Intel that we got is that there's a rogue mercenary group here in the States. They are from all over the world but some of their leaders are German ex- pats raised by a former SS Nazi extremist that slipped into hiding after WWII. They are set on delivering a package of unknown origin, but it involves the Vice President in some way. We know the V.P. will be giving a speech today at the local university. Secret Service has been informed. We're to intercept and assist in capturing the mercenaries that we may find at the event, keep the V.P. safe, and also to bring the group in. Atlas, you will stay with Dr. Monahan so that you can keep us updated if she sees anyone in the crowd that she recognizes. Six and I will be scanning the crowd for any explosive devices. The rest of you will be observing for any suspicious activity."

Atlas looked over at Siobhan and could see the tension building in her eyes. Her brows were pulled together, and her hands stuffed into her pockets. Her golden hair seemed to fall around her shoulders like a halo due to the sunlight coming through windows. He wished he could touch her hair but knew it was too soon, and the timing was all wrong. He moved to stand beside her.

She looked up at him and smiled. "Are you okay?"

"Yeah, you?"

She nodded. "Just worried about Mable."

"Your granddad and Soldier will take great care of her."

She sighed. "I know, but I still worry about her."

"To be honest, I am worried about her and you, too, but she's in good hands, and we have a good team here."

"Of course, you're right."

Instinctively he put his arm around her, as if they had been together always.

She leaned her head against his shoulder.

Atlas took a deep breath, inhaling her unique scent, like honeysuckle and wild flowers.

"Everyone, it's time to move out," Kujo said.

Atlas came out of his little trance and turned to look at Siobhan. "Are you sure you still want to do this? You can back out anytime. We can do this without you, if need be."

"No, I'd feel safer there with you, and also I need to help bring these guys down."

He took her head. "Then let's load up."

CHAPTER 5

THE DRIVE to the event seemed to take forever, and at the same time only seconds. Siobhan had not felt this kind of exhilaration and fear since she'd been in the military. Even though she'd only met Atlas that one time before, and now had spent about 24 hours with him, she felt comfortable with him, like they'd known each other their entire lives.

Taking a quick peek at him from the passenger seat, she noted he always seemed to be in control, and yet there was a casualness about him, an instant sense of ease that drew her to him, just like it had that night six years ago. Just as she started to look away, his hand left the steering wheel and encased her hand, bringing it his knee. His warmth seeped into her and calmed her raw nerves. How did he stay so calm?

"Siobhan, when we're at the event, I want you to stay with me at all times and let me know if you see anyone you recognize from the hospital."

"Alright." She let out a deep sigh. "Atlas, when this is all over, I want to tell Mable that you're her father."

Without taking his eyes from the road, "I'd really like that. I was meaning to ask you if I could spend time with her. If that would be ok with you...?"

She smiled. "I'd really love that, and she seems to have already taken a shine to you. I'm sure the transition to having you in her life won't be that difficult."

"I would also like to spend time with you as well," he said, shooting a quick glance at her.

Not taking her gaze from him, she smiled and nodded her head.

They held hands for the rest of the drive.

As they pulled in to the parking area for the event, all the vehicles that had come with them pulled in next to each other, forming a line of black SUVs. Seemed like the men in black or some ominous government agency had arrived, but to look at these men, you knew that they had all seen things that had forever changed them. They all stood together, Siobhan seemingly the lone stranger amongst them, but she felt their comradery. Sometimes, she wished she'd stayed in the military, because she missed that feeling of belonging to something bigger than herself. But getting out had been what she'd needed to do for her daughter.

KUJO WALKED UP TO THEM, "Lady and gentlemen," he said with a nod in their direction. "You all know the game plan. Each of you take an ear bud—you as well, Siobhan—and report any suspicious activity."

They all acknowledged his order. Siobhan slipped the ear bud into her ear and tested its functionality. When she was sure it worked correctly, she fell in step beside Atlas as they moved toward the crowd of people that was already forming.

There were little booths set up on the outskirts of the field where they were holding the event, and there were volunteers handing out water bottles. She could feel the warmth radiating off of Atlas as he got closer to her and put one arm around her shoulder. Earlier, they had discussed making it seem like they were a couple. It felt so right that she almost put her head on his shoulder but kept herself from making that overly familiar gesture.

"Do you see anything?" he said, leaning close to whisper in her ear.

"Nothing so far, but when I saw them, they were all wearing military gear, so I'll really have to keep my eyes peeled this time."

The crowd moved forward to take seats in front of the stage that had been set in the middle of the university football field.

The ear bud in her ear crackled, and then she heard one of the men's voices say, "Sharpshooter in place, nothing on visual yet."

"Everyone in position?" Kujo asked.

In unison, they all replied, "Roger."

"You know, Atlas," Siobhan said, "this kind of reminds me of being in the military. Now granted, I wasn't in a unit like yours, but all the training we did before deployment was like this."

"Yeah." He nodded with a twisted smile. "Brings back old memories."

She glanced at the Band-Aid she'd affixed to his head. It didn't take away from his naturally alluring physique but seemed to make him less superhuman in a way, more approachable. He looked down at her and his crystal blue eyes seemed to sparkle with mischief.

She giggled under her breath. "You could sweep a girl off her feet with a look like that."

"You better be careful, Doc, or I might just do that," he said with a wink.

They both looked around. More and more people were arriving.

"With all these people here, and more arriving, I hope I'll be able to pick out the mercenaries," she said in a whisper to Atlas.

"Don't worry. The guys are trained what to look for. You're only here for cursory review of the crowd, like the cherry on the top of a sundae."

"Wow, way to make a girl feel appreciated and hungry at the same time."

His deep laugh gave her a warm feeling all the way to her toes. His warmth seeped into her, and she wanted to step closer to him to feel a part of him and all that glorious heat. He moved past her, and she finally came out of her happy daze. Following close behind him, she took his hand when he reached back and felt a warm zing travel up her arm.

Toward the middle of the crowd stood two men talking with their heads together. They both had the hulking build of the men in the hospital and both wore dark clothing. In a crowd of bright colors and summer attire, two men wearing long sleeves and pants stood out.

"Hey, guys," she said, "two suspicious men at my 12 o'clock."

"Roger," came Kujo's voice. "Swede, do you have a visual?"

"Roger," Swede responded. "Moving in."

"Good call, Doc," Kujo said.

Warmth filled Siobhan's chest. "Thanks."

From the side of the crowd off to their left, she saw a flash of red, her gaze drawn to the red like a moth to a flame. The female that had been with the Germans in the hospital had worn red. The person wearing red moved out of sight, and Siobhan stopped to scan the crowd. Farther to the left, she saw another flash of red. With a quick glance further ahead, she saw a tall slender woman with streaming red hair.

Siobhan stepped out, moving fast in the direction of the woman. She tried to not take her eyes off her, but also did not want the woman to see her if she was one of the mercenaries.

"Hey, Siobhan, slow down," Atlas called out.

"I think I recognize that lady," she said, nodding in the woman's direction.

With more determination, Siobhan picked up

speed and ran through the crowd. She narrowly missed running into several people. She continued to follow the woman until she turned between two buildings at the end of the field. The woman's pace slowed enough that Siobhan caught up. When she was close enough, she reached out to tap her shoulder.

The lady in red whipped around.

The two women made eye contact.

Siobhan barely had time to confirm it was the woman from the hospital. With a quick step back, she narrowly missed the other woman's fist. Taking a fighting stance, she raised her arms. The other woman swung her right leg, trying to take Siobhan down with a sweeping kick. With the military training she'd had and the Krav Maga self-defense class she took on a weekly basis, Siobhan was ready.

Sounds of the crowd faded into the background as Siobhan focused on the women in front of her. The redhead darted forward and swung her fist at Siobhan's head.

She ducked beneath the woman's fist and landed a blow against the woman's abdomen then danced away.

The woman came at her again, this time tagging her with a kick against her ribs.

Siobhan's breath left in a hard gust, but she raised her arms in time to deflect the fist that came, aimed at the same side of her body.

Suddenly, the other women clipped Siobhan's chin, and for a moment she saw stars. Furious with herself for leaving her other side open for the blow, Siobhan felt a spike of adrenaline and rushed the woman, taking her to the ground. They wrestled, trading body punches.

Siobhan knew she was in trouble when the woman wriggled and bucked, then flipped them both. She forced Siobhan to her side then clamped a red-clad arm around her neck.

Her vision blurring around the edges, Siobhan gasped for air.

Suddenly, the women in red was gone and another gentler set of strong arms wrapped her. The smell of musky man and the outdoors surrounded her, and a familiar male voice was talking to her. "Siobhan, can you hear me? Siobhan, answer me."

"Yeah," she rasped. "I'm okay." She stared up into Atlas's pale face.

He shook his head. "Doc, you scared the crap out of me."

CHAPTER 6

AFTER LOSING her in the crowd, Atlas had frantically searched, catching glimpses of Siobhan as she'd slipped through the crowd after the woman. A group of people had steeped in front of him and he had to go around then which stole precious seconds in his pursuit of her. Atlas had never been so scared or so impressed in his life. He had just watched the woman he was starting to think of as *his* almost take out what had to be a trained assassin. Within seconds of seeing Siobhan pin the women, she was flipped over and choked, and he could see the life draining from her.

Trying to stay calm, he said into his mic, "Need help, guys."

He took a quick glance over at the women in red, still laying there after he'd knocked her out.

Swede and Kujo came sprinting and put plastic zip ties on the wrists and ankles of the lady in red. Six circled around the men.

Watching the men and the dog, Atlas vowed that, one day, he was going to get a dog, and he wanted to make sure it was good around kids, so his daughter could play with it. Wow, he had a daughter. Life had changed in a heartbeat and Atlas was not going to let go of what he'd found. Squeezing tighter on Siobhan, he heard a mumbled voice.

"Atlas, trouble breathing here, can you give me some room?"

"Sure," he said, easing his hold. But he wouldn't let go, never again.

He helped Siobhan sit up and took stock of all her bruises, his hands roaming over her body as he checked to make sure she was okay.

"Uh, hey, I'm okay," she muttered.

"Just making sure," he said as he put out an arm to help her to stand. A warm shiver went through him when she placed her arm around his waist.

He watched as Siobhan moved to the woman sprawled on the ground.

"I hear something, don't you?" she said, glancing back at him.

"No. Be careful."

She leaned over the woman's body, pulled back her red hair and grasped a white ear bud from the woman's ear. She held it close to her ear, then closed her hand around it and held it away. "Atlas, I hear them speaking German. They're talking about the package... It's the Vice President, and they have a shooter on one of the buildings surrounding the field."

A cold chill shivered down his spine, and he turned to give Kujo a hard stare.

Kujo started talking rapidly into his mic then turned away. "Team, listen up. Reaper cover the eagle's nest and Bear cover the VP's location. We gotta move now. Chatter we picked up from the mercenaries sounds like the package is a sniper. The VP isn't here yet but will be soon."

"What's the call boss?" Atlas came to stand by Kujo and Swede. Siobhan moved next to him, and he reached out to hold her hand.

Kujo shot a glance toward them. "Atlas, Secret Service has been informed, but the V.P. wants to continue on. If the sniper is not found before then, he will leave at the last minute. They are giving us a chance so that the mercs don't know that we know."

"Okay, where do you want us?" Siobhan asked.

Atlas shook his head. "You need to head back to our vehicles and sit tight." He looked into her eyes, saw the fierce frown, as well as her determination and strong will. He felt warmth in his chest and realized he was truly falling for this woman. "Okay, you stay with me, but when this is over, we're going to get you checked out at a hospital."

"Fine."

They turned to Kujo.

"I need you two patrolling the crowd, keeping an eye out for any more of the men you saw in the hospital the other day. Also, I need you to keep listening in on that mic to see if there are any changes to their plans."

Swede stayed behind to guard the woman.

Kujo walked off toward the crowd, giving orders into his mic, calling for police, and letting them know about the woman they'd detained.

Atlas took Siobhan's hand as they walked in the crowd so that they could canvas another area.

"Siobhan, you really scared me over there," he said.

"Sorry. I knew I couldn't let her get away. I just jumped into action."

"Literally," he said, his tone dry.

"Well, I do that in the ER. I just jump into action and get stuff done. I would say that I learned to act like that through the military. But, honestly, my parents and my grandfather raised me that way."

He liked that about her and felt a connection with her because doing something for the greater good was why he'd joined SEAL Team 6 and why he'd gone to work for Hank and the Brotherhood Protectors.

"When this is over, we need to have a serious ice cream party," Siobhan said.

Atlas chuckled. "I think you've lost it."

They stopped in the middle of the crowd. He looked down at her as she turned to stand in front of him. Swiftly he took her in his arms and kissed her. Like a crashing wave, all the emotions swelled over him. Her lips were warm, and her taste was intoxicating. He heard a little moan come from her, and she seemed to sag into his arms, melting into him. She fit against him like a puzzle piece, and he never wanted to let go. But the situation forced them apart.

They broke away from each other, and he watched as she gasped for air just like he was trying to catch his breath. He kept her close but at arm's length.

He heard garbled whispers.

Siobhan let go of him, turned her head slightly, and placed the mercenary ear bud back in her ear. Since he couldn't hear anything on the Brotherhood Protectors mic, she must have been listening to the mercenaries.

She wrapped the earpiece in her hand and said, "Kujo, the sniper is set up in the building third to the right of the podium that the VP is going to take."

In his own mic, Atlas heard, Kujo respond, "This is what we've been waiting for."

For a moment, he didn't hear all the orders Kujo was giving. He couldn't take his gaze off the woman in front of him. He wanted to take her away from there. Get her out of danger.

"Atlas, did you hear me?" Kujo said.

Atlas shook his head and focused on Kujo's words. "Say again."

"I need you and Siobhan to head over to where Swede is standing by the podium. I'll meet you guys over there, shortly."

"Roger," Atlas acknowledged.

As they walked toward the podium, Atlas noticed

more people gathering. As they started to pass more and more people, Siobhan came to a sudden stop.

She cupped the redhead's earpiece to her ear and listened. Once again, she held it away. "Hold on. The Germans are talking again. They're asking for someone to report in."

"Do you think they're asking for the women in red?" he asked.

Siobhan fit the device into her ear again and motioned for him to be quiet. "They're looking for her. She must be in charge or one of the higher ups."

Shouting sounded in his ear piece. On the mic, he heard, "Guys, they've found the sniper and have him subdued. Police are on the way."

"Atlas, you, Siobhan, and anyone else not helping with the sniper, I need you guys watching for any more of the terrorists. Hopefully, they won't try to start anything now that their plan is foiled, but they may make a last-ditch effort."

"Roger," Atlas and Siobhan said in unison.

He looked down at her, and she smiled. He noticed how the sun shone on her hair, and it was paler in the light with strands of red running through the blonde. From what he could remember of seeing Mable's hair, it was the same color. He was so ready for this to be over, so he could spend time with them.

As they walked toward the stage and podium that had been set up for the VP and other special guests, Bear was just ahead of them, already standing to the left of the podium, scanning the area. To their right, Kujo came with his dog Six. On the dog's vest, it said, "Service Dog" and didn't look like the usual tactical gear. They weren't trying to freak anyone out, so the goal was to make things seem normal.

Ahead of them, Secret Service men escorted the VP to the stage, and the crowd surged forward. As this happened, Atlas noticed a large man dressed in black, weaving his way through the crowd at a quick clip.

"Atlas, you see that guy over there, walking through the crowd toward the stage?" Siobhan said in his ear.

"Yeah, I see him," he moved forward. "Stay here."

Not waiting to see if she listened to him, he started walking as fast as he could, without drawing attention to himself, to intercept the terrorist. The man wearing black didn't slow down but seemed to notice that Atlas was coming toward him and picked up speed. Now having to run toward the man, Atlas said, "Guys, there is a man in black heading for the stage and the VP."

As Atlas drew nearer, the other man sprinted to reach the stage, jumped onto it, and ran for the Vice President, raising a large hunting knife with jagged edges in his hand. Atlas leaped onto the stage behind him, tackling him from behind. They rolled.

Atlas's left shoulder hit the podium hard. Air whooshed out of his lungs. He grabbed the other man's arms, trying to keep him from shoving the knife into his chest. All arms and legs, they rolled on the stage. Atlas slammed the man's hand against the ground, shaking the knife loose of his grip.

The mercenary pulled back his fist to punch. Atlas grappled with him, deflecting the hit, but they both were of the same build, tall and bulky. Neither could get an advantage. He heard a woman shout but couldn't turn his attention to see what was happening. Suddenly, the man in black was pulled off him, and Siobhan was there.

She dropped to her knees and pulled him into her arms. "Oh my God, Atlas, are you okay?"

She ran her hands all over his body, and he could feel the blood going down to areas that didn't need to be excited at this moment.

He took her hands in his and felt their warmth,

noting how small they were compared to his. "Sweetheart, I'm fine."

"You should be more careful. Your head...the wound is bleeding again."

She pushed off the ground, and that is when he realized that there were Secret Service men and Brotherhood Protectors surrounding the man he'd fought. They had just finished subduing him. Two of the Secret Service men were walking away with him.

Atlas stood and dusted off his clothing. Another Secret Service agent came up to Atlas, dressed in a black suit, tie and sunglasses.

He stuck out his hand to Atlas. "Thank you for serving our country. If you'll follow me, the Vice President would like to thank you."

Siobhan had mixed feelings about everything that was happening as she followed Atlas to see the VP. They had let Kujo and the other Brotherhood Protectors know where they were headed, while the other guys met with law enforcement. She had heard the men talking, and Atlas was to report to the hospital with Siobhan to get her checked out, and then report to Hank afterward.

The VP was very gracious when they met with

him. He assured them that all the men and Siobhan would be acknowledged later for their valor.

The Secret Service didn't want the VP to stick around after that and whisked him away in his black sedan.

When it was all over and they were walking across the field to their vehicle, Siobhan said, "Atlas, you know you're crazy."

"What do you mean?" He gave her a wink and draped an arm around her shoulders. When they reached the vehicle, he turned her around, and his lips descended to claim hers.

Warmth spread throughout her whole body. She hadn't felt anything like this in years. Since before Mable had been born.

Atlas's arms encircled her body, pulling her close.

Siobhan's knees would have given out, had he not been holding her tight.

He brought her body against his, and they seemed to meld into one person. After several long minutes of a soulful kiss, they drew away from each other, both gasping for air.

Atlas retained his hold around her middle, but they both leaned back slightly.

"We'd better head to the hospital now," he said, giving her one more quick kiss.

He turned, not letting go of her, and opened the door to help her slide into the SUV.

She watched as he walked around the vehicle and got in on the driver's side.

"Doc, which way do we go to get to the closest hospital?" he asked. Atlas steered them onto the main road and turned left onto the highway. The directions she gave him were to the hospital where she worked. Suddenly, the last couple of days slammed into her like a brick to her chest. She hadn't shown up for work that day, and she'd been on the schedule.

"Don't worry, Doc. Hank called your hospital and let them know that there was an emergency, and that's why you left. He talked to your boss directly and let him know the basic details. There won't be any repercussions. They're expecting you back Monday."

"When did you find out about that?"

"When we were at the bunker this morning, I checked in with Hank."

The drive seemed to fly past. Before she knew it, they were pulling up to the hospital.

She showed him the nurse's station and introduced him to her nurses. One of them checked him out then turned to wink at Siobhan. She smiled at her and motioned that she'd tell her more later. They walked to the room toward the back so that they could have one of the other ER docs to check them over in private.

"Ahhh, Dr. Monahan, we were wondering when we'd see you again," the doctor said, smiling.

"It has been a little crazy, and we've both had a few injuries. Atlas has hit his head on the side of a cave, yesterday, and got a cut when he tackled a man today. Probably just a few bruises, but I would like to get a CT of his head just to be on the safe side."

The doctor pulled back the bandage. "Yes, I see. Very nice stitching, Dr. Monahan."

He motioned for Atlas to sit on the table in the small emergency room. He stretched out his hand to Atlas. "My name's Dr. Hughes."

"Very nice to meet you. You can call me Atlas."

"Ah, the Titan that holds all up perpetually." The doctor nodded. "Very interesting. Please, take a seat and let me check out your head. Any headaches or double vision?"

Dr. Hughes pointed a light into Atlas's eyes and had him follow his index finger. "I don't see any issues. Eyes are tracking well, and no headache or vision issues. I don't think we need a CT."

Siobhan nodded and let out a deep sigh.

Atlas jumped off the examination table. "You're up, Doc," he said with a wink at her.

Siobhan walked over to the step that was pulled out from the examination bed, climbed up, and turned around to sit.

Dr. Hughes grinned. "Dr. Monahan, please do tell, what happened to you?"

Clearing her throat, she said, "I fought and tackled another woman to the ground, and then was choked until I started to see stars."

Dr. Hughes's eyes widened. "Very interesting."

He pointed the penlight into her eyes, and she followed his index finger as instructed.

"Do you have any shortness of breath or any pain in your neck?"

"No."

He had her lift her head up to inspect her neck, and he palpated her lymph nodes and around the base of her neck. "Everything looks good. You'll have some bruising around your throat starting tomorrow, but otherwise, you look fine."

"That's good to hear," Atlas said.

"Folks, you will both live," Dr. Hughes announced. "Check out with the nurse at the front desk, and you're done."

Atlas took Siobhan's arm then turned back to the doctor. "Thank you, Dr. Hughes."

"Yes, thank you," Siobhan said. "I'll see you in a few days."

They walked down the hallway arm in arm. Just being next to Atlas seemed to warm her up inside and out. After only a few steps, they were at the nurse's station checking out. She hugged a few of the nurses and reassured them she was fine and would see them in a few days.

Once they were in the car and on their way back to the bunker, Siobhan finally spoke. "Atlas, I do really want you in our lives, in any way that is possible, but let's get Mable settled before we talk about it, okay?"

"Sounds perfect to me. I don't want to upset your lives. I just want to be an addition, if at all possible. And I would love to be a part of Mable's and your lives."

Time seemed to fly as they headed out of town, heading back toward the forest and the bunker that held her family and Soldier. It seemed like a month since she'd last seen them, not just a day. All too soon, the road turned to forest dirt, and they pulled up at the same little clearing and the rock they'd hidden behind just yesterday.

Atlas came up beside her and took her hand as they made their way across to the cave and down through the cavern to the bunker entrance.

"Here we are again," he said, raising his brows.

Just then, the door opened, and her grandfather was there with a stern expression.

Siobhan launched herself at his chest and was engulfed in a bear hug.

"Girl, I'm so glad you're back in one piece."

Out of nowhere, she was almost knocked over by a blonde tornado. "Momma, you're back. What happened? Are you okay? We played dolls and read books, and then Pops made me take a nap."

"Goodness, Mable." Siobhan laughed. "Let's get inside, and we will tell you all about it."

Atlas cleared his throat. "You guys go on in and get your stuff together. I'll debrief Soldier, and then we can head out."

"Will do," said her grandfather.

She paused before entering the bunker with her family, turning back for a moment to see Soldier and Atlas talking. Atlas had his cellphone out, and they were walking toward the entrance of the cave, probably to get better cell service. Kujo had told Atlas to call Hank and give an update. Facing forward again, she stepped into the bunker, behind her daughter and grandfather.

"Little priss, can you start cleaning up your stuff, and then get your bags together? I'll come help you in a minute."

"Yes, Momma."

When she walked away, Siobhan gave her grandfather a smile. "Pops, thank you for keeping an eye on Mable for me."

"You know I'm always here for my girls, and it's not like I'm going anywhere." He raised his eyebrows. "Are we going home now?"

"Yeah, the danger was...taken care of. Atlas is going to make sure we're settled for the night back at home. After that, I'm not sure what's going to happen."

"You like him, don't you?" he asked, his voice gruff.

"What?"

"I can tell. And he's Mable's father, isn't he? He seems like a solid person. You should give him chance."

"Thanks for the advice, Pops." She bared her teeth at him in a forced smile, but then came over to hug him. "I don't know what we would do without you. You're our glue."

He looked away briefly, but she could see he was getting choked up. If it hadn't been for her grandfather, she would have truly struggled raising her daughter and working at the same time. Not all families had that kind of support, and since he was all she had left, they stuck together to keep each other out of trouble. From across the room, she saw Mable struggling to push the toy bin, with toys still hanging out of it, under her cot.

Siobhan rushed across the room. "My little sweet, do you need help?"

"No, I got it, Momma."

"Hold on, let me straighten this out, and then we can close the lid and put it under your bed, okay?"

Moving the lid and some of the toys around, she replaced the lid, and then waited as her daughter shoved it under the bed.

From behind her, a deep voice startled her. "Are y'all ready? I'm taking you home."

CHAPTER 7

SHE SHOVED the few things she'd brought with her into her overnight bag, making sure to grab her favorite brush. The whole time she kept an eye on Atlas. Every time she looked at him, she admired all his muscles and how they moved under his skin. Just looking at him gave her warm tingles, and she wanted to know if it still felt as good to make love with him as it had six years ago. With some regret, she pushed those thoughts aside to help her daughter pack her favorite blanket and the toy that she'd brought with her.

When she was done, she turned to her grandfather. "Pops, are you ready to go?"

He rolled his eyes. "You know I am. I'm just waiting on you girls."

He pulled Mable under his arm with a little sideways hug and took her overnight bag. The bag was pretty large for such a little girl, but Siobhan knew he had tried to make Mable feel comforted and had probably grabbed whatever the little girl had wanted to bring. Bending over to lift her own bag, she was surprised when Atlas came in and swooped her bag off the floor.

"I can take this, if you don't mind," he said.

His clear blue eyes that matched Mable's shone back at and her, and for a moment she was mesmerized. "If you are so inclined, be my guest," she said with a huge grin.

They only kept the basics in the bunker, like extra tooth brushes and toothpaste, but she had packed her blow dryer and makeup, with extra clothes for work and regular day-to-day clothes. Her bag was not light. Atlas hefted it onto his shoulder as though it weighed no more than a feather.

She giggled. "Well, macho-man, don't stop me."

"After you, milady," he said with a little bow.

She could tell he said it as a joke, but there was also a hint of possessiveness. "Milady" meant *his* lady.

They all trooped out to the SUVs. One had been hidden in the secret lean-to her grandfather had built, and then he'd further disguised the vehicle with bushes and a camouflage tarp he'd stashed there previously. Pop decided to ride with Soldier. They were having too much fun exchanging "war stories." Atlas drove Siobhan and Mable in the rental.

The drive was quiet for Atlas and Siobhan, but Mable watched a kiddie movie that had been set up on her tablet, entertaining her for the entire ride back home. At some time during the trip, Siobhan's daughter fell asleep, her head lolling onto the door of the car with her little blanket under chin. If Siobhan had tried sleeping like that now, she would have the worst crick in her neck.

Atlas cleared his throat. "Hank and I think it would be a good idea for Brotherhood Protectors to stay for a few more days to make sure there's no more trouble."

"That's fine," she said, her heartbeat kicking up. "We can put you up in the guest room. Do you think Soldier would be okay bunking with you? Or we can put him on the foldout couch in the den?"

"No, when we get back, Soldier is taking a cab to the airport so he can catch a commercial flight back to Brotherhood headquarters. He already has his next mission set up."

Her heart beat faster. Atlas would be staying alone with her family. "Since it's the weekend now, we can get settled back at home before we have to go back to school and work."

"Roger that."

Trees on either side of the road changed to city buildings as they took the turn off toward the edge of the city where her home nestled in the suburbs. He already had her address in the GPS, so she didn't have to give him directions.

Soon after, they turned down her street. He pulled into the driveway behind her grandfather who parked his car in his spot inside the garage. They would need to make sure they picked her vehicle up from downtown wherever Hank had arranged for it to be stored. Hopefully, it was safe. "We'll have to get my car sometime this weekend."

"One of the Brothers picked it up for you. They left it at the rental company. We can get it when we turn this one in."

Siobhan shook her head with a smile. "Dang, your team thinks of everything."

"We do try to think of every contingency," he said with a quick grin.

They both got out of the car at the same time and went around to the trunk to retrieve the bags. Atlas grabbed both of her bags and his before she got a chance to get hers out. She guided him to the garage door entrance that led into the house.

Pops was already sending Mable upstairs to her room, her bag abandoned at the bottom of the stairs. "You kids get settled. I'll have supper ready in about an hour."

"Thanks, Pops." she leaned over and gave him a peck on his cheek. Then she turned to the tall man beside her. "Follow me, Atlas."

Moving around her grandfather, she motioned Atlas to follow her up the stairs. They passed Mable who was already playing with her dolls and horses on the floor in her room. Siobhan's bedroom was down the hall on the right with her grandfather on the left. The guest room was down the hall on the left past Mable's room.

"This will be your room while you're here," she said, opening the door and stepping aside. "There's a guest bathroom just past your room on the right."

"Where is your room?"

He was standing just behind her when she turned to respond, and if she had moved half an inch, her chest would've rubbed against his.

He stepped into the room, placed the bags on the floor, and then his arms came around her before she could think. His lips descended to hers and their bodies moved together.

Heat surged from every place he touched her. She sighed into his mouth, and when her lips parted, his tongue delved inside her. She opened wider and let her tongue explore the interior of his mouth. He had a musky flavor she wanted to continue to explore but was startled when he moved deeper into the room, walking her backwards until her legs touched the edge of the bed. His hands roamed over her body, and she was distracted again. His fingers found her nipples through her clothing, and she leaned against him.

She broke her mouth from his momentarily. "Hold on," she said, panting. "I need to close the door."

When she looked, the door was already closed.

He arched an eyebrow then kissed her again, chuckling against her mouth. "Don't worry so much. I know you want your privacy, and I'm keeping an ear out for Mable as well."

She sighed again and went back into his arms. His roaming hands began unbuttoning her shirt. One arm was freed from a sleeve, and then the other. Just a bra kept the top of her body from being completely exposed while her jeans were still on.

Strong well-muscled arms encircled her torso while he continued to kiss her jaw and neck. Then he unhooked her bra. Her breasts sprang from the cups.

Atlas leaned down and took a nipple into his mouth and suckled.

Siobhan arched her back as Atlas held her in his muscled arms while he continued to lavish her breast with attention. He gently laid her over the bed with her legs over the edge of the mattress then shifted his mouth to her neglected breast while he unbuttoned her jeans. The jeans seemed to stick to her hips, but he gave them a tug and dropped to the floor.

Siobhan smoothed her hands over his chest and his washboard abs. She roamed upward, shoving up his shirt.

He released her breast and pulled his shirt over his head. "Sweetheart, move onto the bed."

"Okay," she said, feeling like teenager who was being naughty. A giggle escaped her lips.

"Your body is like a candy. I want to lick until I find out how many licks it takes to get to the center." He prowled her body, moving down her torso to her hips. He pushed open her legs so that her knees were spread and bent slightly.

"I don't know how many licks it'll take," he rasped, "but I'm willing to find out."

He bent over her sex and settled between her legs. His hands swept up the inner part of her thighs, and she watched as his face came closer to her center. A warm tongue touched her, and she almost came off the bed. His arms gripped her legs, and she tried to stifle a moan.

"Ohhh, Atlas don't stop."

He focused all of his attention on her sweet spot, his tongue moving faster and delving deeper. Spirals of warmth and electric tingles spread from where his tongue was making magic.

Her breathing grew faster and sharper, and just before she thought she'd split into a million pieces, he stopped.

Siobhan blinked open her eyes to find him suddenly on top of her.

He groaned. "Give me one second. I have to get a condom."

"Aw, what?" she asked, slightly dazed.

He jumped off the bed, riffled through his bag, and pulled out a silver packet. Quickly, he ripped it open and rolled the condom down his penis, and then was back on top of her before she could unglue her tongue from the roof of her mouth.

"Sorry about that," he muttered.

"Glad you're back," she said, then felt her lips spread in a huge grin.

His mouth captured hers again, and she felt the tip of his cock touch her pulsating core, but then he moved away again.

"Oh God, don't stop," she said, and dug her nails into his backside.

This time, he drove his cock deep, and with so much force she arched off the bed.

"Siobhan, honey, are you okay?" he asked, his jaw clenching. "I'm so sorry. I got a little carried away."

She blew a breath between her pursed lips. "Don't stop, Atlas. Keep going...you feel so good." She met his next thrust, rolling her hips upward to meet him.

They set a pounding rhythm, both frenzied, and meeting in harsh thrusts, as if they couldn't get close enough to each other. She felt her body spiraling again, and the burning deep in her core was a flame. The faster she moved, the faster he pounded into her body. Finally, she couldn't hold on any longer, and she felt herself shatter into a million pieces.

Atlas jerked then held. His cock pulsed inside her. Then he lowered his body onto hers while he dragged in deep breaths. His weight felt good and real. She hoped she'd have more time with this man who already seemed so integral to her life though it had only been a few days.

Atlas rolled off her body but brought her with him so that she was now on top, sprawled over his muscular frame. Her breasts were pressed into the short hairs of his chest, and they slightly tickled her nipples. She felt and heard a rumble in his body.

He chuckled. "I guess I'm a little hungry."

She raised her head and pushed back her hair. "Don't worry. My grandfather makes the best food. You'll think he's a professional."

"Having something home-cooked will be a nice change, for sure."

He leaned up to her and gave her forehead a swift peck of his lips, and then turned slightly so that she was laying on the bed and as his cock slid from her body. He stood, rolled off the condom and then used his shirt to clean up. On his way back to the bed, he leaned over to pick up his underwear and jeans. The fly of his jeans was still open as he came up between Siobhan's legs where she sat at the edge of the bed. The denim rubbed against the tender skin of her thighs and another moan escaped her lips. Leaning toward her, he wrapped her legs around his torso, lifted her off the bed, and took her lips in a passionate kiss. As good as that kiss was, she knew they needed to get back downstairs.

When he pulled back, she scrunched her nose.

He sighed. "We need to get downstairs before someone comes looking, don't we?"

She nodded, making a face.

He placed her back on the floor, but she swayed slightly and clung to his waist. Atlas tipped her head up with his index finger. "Siobhan, I'm here now, and whatever we need to do, I want to spend time with you. Everything will fall into place, okay?"

"You promise?"

"Yes, now get dressed before I ravage you again."

She giggled then grabbed her clothes and shoved her limbs back into all the appropriate holes. Just as she finished zipping and buttoning, Atlas opened the door. There in the hallway was Mable with a doll in her hand.

"Pops says supper is ready," she said.

"Thanks, sweetie," Siobhan said. "We'll be right behind you. Lead the way."

Atlas came up behind Mable and swooped her up in his arms. "What is this—a little airplane? Vroom." He swung her under his arm and made airplane noises down the stairs while Mable giggled and squealed.

"That was fun. Can we do it again?" she said when they reached the bottom.

"We can later, little bean," he said, "but let's go help set the table."

"Yippee! Did you hear that, Pops? We're going to be airplanes later."

"Well, that will be fun," Siobhan's grandfather said. "Now, set the table. All the silverware is on the side of the table. Let your momma get the knives."

Atlas sat at the table with his family; what an amazing sight he had before him. He knew this was a tenuous thing, and that he would need to show Siobhan, her grandfather and little Mable that he would be there for them. He'd never bought a home before, so he could go anywhere, but he really needed to settle down, and now, he had a reason to put down roots.

"Atlas, how long are they planning for you to stay?" Pat asked.

"Not sure, sir, but Hank said for at least a few days," Atlas said. "Honestly, I'd like to stick around longer to get to know my girls."

Everyone at the table except Mable stopped midbite to stare at him.

Pat tilted his head. "Son, what are your intentions?"

"Pops, please," Siobhan whispered.

Atlas waved a hand. "No, it's okay, Siobhan. You all have a right to know." Turning back to her grandfather, he said, "Sir, I want to be a part of Mable's life, and if Siobhan will let me, I would like to date her. My hope is that, one day, maybe we could make an official family of this."

From the corner of his eye, he saw Siobhan's mouth drop open, and Mable had stopped what she was doing and was staring at him as well.

"I'm glad to hear it," Pat said, and started eating his food again.

Siobhan and Mable continued to stare at Atlas. He finally glanced over and smiled at them, and then winked.

Mable giggled and scooped up a spoonful of food.

Siobhan mouthed across the table at him that they would talk later.

The fork in his hand sunk into the steak on his plate, when suddenly he felt a foot kick him in the shin. He looked across the table at Siobhan, who smiled at him with a little gleam in her green eyes.

He raised his eyebrows at her, and then continued to eat his steak with gusto.

The rest of the meal was filled with small talk. After they were finished eating, they all shuffled their plates to the sink, and while Pat and Siobhan put away the food, Atlas and Mable cleaned the dishes.

"Mable, you are a pro at doing dishes," Atlas said. "I think you may have been doing this for twenty years."

Mable giggled. "No, silly, I just learned how this year."

He made sure to keep all the knives away from her and only give her one item at a time. For such a young little person, she was very diligent about doing a good job. The plates were almost as big as Mable's torso, but she handled them very carefully. Already, he felt pride at how amazing she was. Pat and Siobhan were doing a wonderful job raising her.

Siobhan came up beside Mable to help her to put the silverware and dishes on the rack before they had towel-dried them by hand. They worked an assembly line. Pat finished what he was doing, and Atlas saw him wink and walk off to leave them alone. He was giving Atlas the "okay" to be a part of the family.

"What do you think, Momma?" Mable said, glancing at Siobhan.

"About what?"

"Is it okay if Atlas stays, so we can play, and he can date you?"

Atlas smiled down at his daughter. He knew that he couldn't call her that quite yet, but she was his, and he would die for her.

"What do you think, Mable?" her mother asked. "Would you like that?"

"Yes, Momma, I would like for Atlas to stay." She grinned up at Atlas.

He bent over, laid a smooch on her check, and then pulled her up and swung her gently into his arms, being careful not to swing her into anything. She squealed then put her arms around him for a big little-girl bearhug. Atlas though his heart was going to break from how much joy he felt. With a quick step to the right, he put his arm around Siobhan and brought them in for a group hug. Not wanting to let go of them, he squeezed them to his chest, the smells of honeysuckle from Siobhan and Play-doh and little girl wafted over him.

When he released them, he said, "Girls, what would you ladies like to do tonight?"

"I wanna watch a movie," Mable said.

"What do you want to watch?" he asked.

Still carrying Mable on his left side and holding Siobhan under his right arm, they moved to the living room. Mable squirmed, and he put her down on the floor as he disengaged from Siobhan. The little girl sprinted across the room and collapsed on the floor in front of the TV stand with all the movies on it.

From where Atlas stood, it seemed like they owned every Disney movie ever made. "Wow, that's quite a collection you girls have there."

Mable jumped up, came over to Atlas, and grabbed his arm to pull him over to the movies. "Which one is your favorite?"

"Hmm." He tapped his chin. "When I was a kid, I really liked Disney's *Robin Hood*. Do you have that one?"

"We have that one," Mable exclaimed. "I like when the snake drinks the special juice and acts all silly."

"Yes, that's my favorite part, too," he said and looked up at Siobhan. They winked at each other.

The movie was put in the player, and they all settled on the couch together, Mable under his left arm and Siobhan cuddled against him on his right. Before the movie was over, Mable had fallen asleep and Atlas started dozing off. Siobhan nudged him and pointed at their little girl and then up to her room.

He nodded. Siobhan pushed off the sofa, and Atlas pulled Mable up against his chest and rose. Together, they headed up the stairs. They went to their daughter's room. He entered a pink and purple whimsical room. The little bed was off to the left. He placed Mable on the bed and pulled the blankets up around her.

Siobhan leaned around his shoulder and whispered into his ear, "She's the sweetest angel."

"Just like her mother."

She moved into his arms, and they shared a quiet gentle kiss.

Atlas drew a deep breath. "I'm falling in love with you all."

EPILOGUE

One year later...

"Atlas, where are the keys to my Subaru?" Siobhan asked.

"They should be in your handbag."

"I don't see them," she called out. "Hurry, I need your help. We have to go."

"I'm coming."

From the other side of the kitchen, Atlas came in, carrying Mable under one arm with her grandfather trailing behind them. "Uh oh, what is this creature in my arms? Is it a bear?"

"No," Mable said. A little meow came from her.

"Ahhh, a lion?" he guessed.

"Yes!" she said, as she squirmed from his arms and he placed her on the floor. She pushed her hair out of her face and looked up at Siobhan. "Hi, Momma, we were playing zoo."

"That's nice," Siobhan said, smiling. "Are you ready so we can go see if we're going to have your brother today?"

"Yippee," she squealed and ran around the kitchen.

Atlas caught her up in his arms again and threw her over his shoulder.

"We're ready. Did you find your keys?" he said with a wink as he pulled the jangling keys from his pocket.

She arched a brow. "Uh huh, so that's where they were."

They all piled into her SUV to go to her OB/GYN appointment to see if she could be induced today. Siobhan couldn't believe all that had happened in the last year. Atlas had tried to court her, but they'd realized very quickly that they were meant to be, so he transferred and worked for the Brotherhood Protectors from Seattle.

They'd been married now for about 8 months.

They had a cute little wedding and, of course, taken Mable and Pat on their honeymoon. They'd wanted their entire family together, so it hadn't felt like a burden.

While on their honeymoon in a cabin at Yosemite National Park, Siobhan had realized that she was very tired, and her breasts were larger and sore. She knew what those symptoms meant, and when she'd missed her period, she'd taken a pregnancy test. They realized that she must have gotten pregnant pretty quickly, likely during the first few days Atlas had been back in her life.

Siobhan carried low this time and, from the ultrasound they'd had a few months ago, they knew they were having a boy. They all piled into her full-size SUV; with new family members came bigger vehicles. Siobhan was helped into the passenger seat by Atlas. Her grandfather got Mable and himself buckled into the back. Atlas came around to the driver's side, buckled in and turned to her with his glorious smile, "Ready to meet our son?"

"Hopefully he'll be just like his daddy," Siobhan said.

"I think this one will have red hair like his momma." Atlas winked.

"Hear, hear," said Pat from the back seat.

"I'm just glad we're all together," Siobhan said and smiled back at Atlas.

"On to the next adventure," he said as they pulled out of the drive way and headed to the hospital.

HOT COLORADO NIGHTS

Hot COLORADO Nights

PAIGE YANCEY

BROTHERHOOD PROTECTORS

CHAPTER 1

THE BACK-DOOR light shone down on the porch with an eerie, yellow glow. Maddie Finley shivered, the hairs on the back of her neck rising to attention. Something wasn't right. With the house key in her hand, she walked to the door and pressed her key into the lock. Even before she twisted it, the door swung open, as if blown by a breeze. In that moment, all of Captain Charles E. Finley's, A.K.A. "Dad's", training raced through her mind. She stiffened, her muscles flexing, ready to move.

Maddie dug in her brown leather bag for the heavy-duty flashlight her father insisted she carry. With the device in hand, she eased the purse to the ground beside the red door she and her sister Janie had painted just last month. Fully alert, Maddie flipped on her flashlight and slipped through the entrance.

Something had happened; Maddie could feel it. Her heart thudded hard against her ribs. Where was Janie? A sense of urgency pushed her forward.

When growing up with a single parent and a younger sister, being trained as one of Dad's *troops* hadn't seemed unusual for the two little girls. Back then, it had been a game. Now, as an independent single woman, Maddie knew she was capable of handling anything that might happen because of her Dad's training games.

She tiptoed through the entry hallway into the kitchen, passing the small dining room table. The dinette was just the right size for two adult women who kept busy schedules. The table held the usual, everyday clutter, and nothing was out of place. As she crept further into the house, she could see a dim light glowing from the corridor that led to the bedrooms and shared bathroom.

Where was LouLou, the sisters' spoiled golden retriever? Normally, the big dog attacked the women when they came home at the end of their day, showering them with sloppy wet licks on their cheeks. And then she heard it. Pitiful whining and frantic barking sounded from the bathroom.

Maddie moved slowly, but steadily, her gaze taking in the living area with its cream walls and floors and brown leather chairs. Lamps lay on the floor, tipped off the end tables, and couch cushions were scattered throughout the room. The T.V. had been smashed, and everything in the room looked as if someone had been in a scuffle, and then left in a hurry. From her quick perusal, nothing seemed to have been taken from the room.

Maddie's steps quickened as she entered the hallway and shined her light into her bedroom. Nothing had been touched. The room appeared exactly as she'd had left it that morning before leaving for work.

LouLou's paws scraped against the bathroom door, and she whined to get out.

Maddie's chest tightened. The poor dog was probably frightened and in need of reassurance. If only dogs could talk, then Maddie would know what had happened tonight.

She turned to her left and stood at the entrance to her sister's room, shining her light inside. The room was messier than her sister's everyday clutter. Clothes lay across the floor. Bed pillows and her comforter had been slung from the bed, and her dresser, which usually displayed all her colorful jewelry, was swept clean of all of its items. Then she saw the wall and gasped. Directly across from Maddie, about the height that Janie would have stood, was a dent in the wall with a red smudge in it. Her heart stuttering, Maddie turned back to the bathroom and opened the door.

LouLou leaped out, whining and wiggling, so happy to see Maddie, she couldn't stop moving.

Maddie knelt in front of the dog and hugged her neck, fending off the long swipes of the dog's tongue. "LouLou, baby, what happened? Where's Janie?"

The dog paused in mid-wiggle and ran toward Janie's bedroom. As she entered, she growled, the hairs on the scruff of her neck rising. She sniffed at all the items on the floor, one at a time, before returning to Maddie and sitting at her feet. The retriever stared up at her, her brown eyes appearing full of questions.

Maddie leaned down and patted the dog's soft, velvety head and then reached into her back pocket for her cellphone. "I sure wish you could tell me what happened here, but, for now, we're going to have to call 911 to get some help." After entering the three numbers, she placed the phone to her ear and prayed for a swift response.

. . .

ADAMSTOWN POLICE DETECTIVE Derek Lewis drove up to the house with its nicely cut green grass and wide, welcoming porch graced by two white rocking chairs, sitting like sentinels beside the front door. He shook his head and shifted into Park. No matter how tranquil they looked on the outside, bad things could happen in nice houses, too. The detective stepped out of his standard black sedan and hurried to the front of the house.

Two police cruisers were parked on the road in front, their rotating lights flashing red and blue against the grey stone exterior of the house. The door stood open. He entered. To start the investigation, his job was to talk to the occupants of the home. When he'd been assigned to the case, he'd recognized the name of the 911 caller. How many women named Maddie Finley could there be in the area? His pulse quickened as he strode into the living room and looked into the familiar gaze of the female talking to the police officer. He remembered those crystal blue eyes as if it had only been yesterday. His years on the high school football team came flooding back. Maddie had been his high school sweetheart. Somehow, he'd lost contact with her when he'd left for college.

Sweet Maddie had matured from the gangly

youth he remembered to this curvaceous woman standing before him. Rich brown hair hung loosely down her back. Set in her heart-shaped face, her eyes where the blue of clear water with flecks of turquoise, like tropical island bays, darker now with concern over her missing sister. She stood straight, her brows rising as he approached, but she didn't appear to recognize him.

Derek held out his hand. "Ma'am, my name is Detective Derek Lewis. If you don't mind, I have a few questions for you."

She nodded and turned to the short, older officer she'd been talking to. "Is that all you need from me?"

"Yes, ma'am." He folded his notepad and left the house.

Maddie walked toward Derek with a confidence he'd never seen in her in high school. The top of her head came up to his shoulders. She seemed so small and fragile, making him want to comfort her and let her know he'd help in any way he could. As she drew near, her eyes narrowed.

Maddie gasped, "Derek? Oh my God, it's you."

Derek nodded. "It's good to see you, Maddie. I wish it was under better circumstances."

Maddie reached out her hand to shake his.

When their fingers touched, a shock of heat raced through Derek's body.

Maddie let out a soft gasp, jerked her hand free, and then stepped back slightly.

"When—" A touch of huskiness tinged Derek's voice. He cleared his throat. "When was the last time you saw your sister?"

"At the shop we own, around two o'clock this afternoon," she said. "She left early to get ready for a date."

"With?"

She shook her head. "I don't know."

"When you arrived home, did you notice anything out of place or not as it should be?"

Maddie recited everything she'd told the police officer, starting from when she'd arrived home to when she'd called 911.

At that moment, a golden retriever with a pink collar bounded into the room and sat on its haunches before Derek, looking up with soulful brown eyes.

Derek grinned, reached down and scratched behind her ears. "Is she your dog?"

Maddie looked down with a tight smile. "Janie and I got her a few years ago. She isn't much of a guard dog. She's more of a companion." When she looked up, there were tears shimmering in her eyes and on the verge of falling.

Derek's heart skipped a beat, and he began to lift his hand to give her some comfort, but then let it drop to his side. "Yeah, I love dogs. When I was a kid, we had a beagle. My apartment building doesn't allow pets, so, none for now."

She gave him a weak smile. "Have you heard anything about my sister?"

Derek took a deep breath and captured Maddie's gaze. "We have a report that she was seen on campus getting into a blue 4x4 truck."

Maddie swallowed hard. A single tear escaped and trailed down her cheek. "She told me she was going on a blind date with a guy she met online through her college dating service. Janie should already be home by now. She doesn't stay out late when she goes on dates." Maddie gave him a watery smile. "She stuck with old habits from back when my Dad had us home early from our dates when we were teens."

"Do you mind if I look around?"

She waved him toward the living room. "Please. Do whatever it takes to find her."

He spent several minutes searching each room for clues. What he saw in the bedroom wasn't reassuring. He figured the bloodied dent in the drywall had been the product of someone throwing someone else against the wall with a significant amount of force. If it had been Maddie's sister Janie, the woman could have been knocked out.

When he was finished, Derek turned to find Maddie standing behind him, her eyes rounded, hopeful.

"I don't suppose the living room and her bedroom looked like this before she left on her date?" he asked, knowing the answer.

Maddie shook her head. "She's messy, but this—" She gulped and covered her mouth with her hand, tears welling in her eyes.

With reluctance, he said, "There appears to have been a struggle in here and in the living room. My guess is that your sister was removed from this house by force. We would have treated this as a breaking and entering case. But because of the dent and blood on the wall, we will pursue this as a violent crime and potential abduction."

A sob escaped Maddie's lips, and she buried her face in her hands.

Derek fought the urge to take her into his arms and comfort her. If he hoped to find Maddie's sister, he had to act fast. The first twenty-four hours were critical. "We've had several reports of women being kidnapped over the past six months. We don't have any leads on who's doing it, but some of the women used a dating website, others had gone out on blind dates. Do you know anything else about the man your sister was going to meet?"

At that moment, LouLou whined and started toward the kitchen. She stopped and glanced over her shoulder at Maddie with a baleful look.

Maddie shook her head. "Sorry, LouLou needs to be fed. Most nights we feed her as soon as we get home in the evening. If you don't mind, I'll be right back."

Instead of waiting for her return, Derek followed her into the kitchen.

The golden retriever danced around a white cabinet with bronze-colored handles under the sink.

"Come here, you silly dog, I know you're starving, girl. I just wish that Janie was here." Maddie looked up at Derek as he walked into the kitchen behind her.

"Do you know who Janie hangs out with on campus?" he asked.

Maddie scooped up a container of food from the large bag of dog food and dumped it into a pink metal bowl.

The dog gobbled the kibble as if she was starving, scattering food across the floor.

Maddie stood and straightened her royal-blue, silk blouse over her skinny jeans. "I only know that Janie was going out to dinner to meet this guy. I think she said his name was Caleb. She did mention something about possibly going to a movie after dinner, but that she would call if they did. If they didn't go to a movie, she was to be home by midnight. Janie is very independent, but we look out for each other."

With a nod, Derek turned away and paced the length of the kitchen, and then slowly turned back to her. "Have you met any of the men she's recently dated?"

Maddie shook her head.

"Has she ever used this dating website before?"

With a grimace, Maddie shook her head again. "She lets me know where they're going, and only tells me more details about the guys once she's seeing them on a regular basis. We're both private people, but we're really close. We know what's going on in each other's lives. Mainly, we work together in our store, and she goes to her college classes."

"Has she been involved in drugs?"

Maddie jerked her head up, a frown denting her

brow. "Janie?" She shook her head. "She's a rule-follower. We get that from our dad. Daddy would have found out if we'd tried to get away with anything. Drugs are out of the question."

Derek ran a hand through his hair and glanced around the room, noticing pictures of Maddie and Janie smiling, probably on vacation in what appeared to be France and Italy. The warm golden colors throughout the kitchen and the photographs indicated the two women who lived there were happy and enjoyed life. Derek, also noticed that everything inside the kitchen seemed to come in twos, and looked well-used and cared for. The sisters were a team. They loved each other.

A pang of regret filled Derek's chest. He'd never had a close connection with his siblings. He shook off the feeling and glanced back at Maddie. "Did she give you an alternative number to call or any other information that could help us find the guy she went out with?"

Maddie's eyes narrowed. "I don't think—" Then her eyes brightened. She dug in her back pocket and pulled out her cellphone. "Janie texted me a phone number and an address of where the man lived in case he brought her to his house later. She's always really good about getting this data from the guys she sees and won't go out with them unless they give her this information for security reasons. Dad always grilled us about the guys we would see when we were in high school, so it's like second nature for us now."

He jotted down the information from Janie's text message, and then strode through the interior door to where the officers milled about the living room. He handed his notepad to one of the policemen. "Hey, Joe, call in this address and phone number. Have a unit sent over to check out this location."

The police officer nodded and spoke into his radio, while walking out the door to his cruiser.

Derek made another pass through the home, searching for any other clues he might have missed on the first time through. He wanted to find Maddie's sister. The sooner, the better, for Janie's sake.

MADDIE STOOD at the door to the kitchen and watched Derek as he first talked with the police officer, and then moved about the house, studying the disrupted furniture.

The detective moved with the confidence of experience and knowledge. His well-muscled legs and broad shoulders were leaner than when he'd been in high school, but were more defined after years of working out. He wore a light blue, button-up dress shirt and black, fitted slacks as well as black leather shoes. His hair was cut in a short to medium length, with the front being somewhat longer. When he brushed his hands through his hair, it stood straight up.

For a few minutes, he disappeared into Janie's bedroom.

Maddie fought the urge to follow him, knowing he needed the space to work through the clues. She waited in the kitchen doorway, trying not to freak out. Her sister needed her to be calm, to remember anything that might be of use in the effort to find her.

After a few minutes, Derek strode back down the hallway to where she stood. "I'll need her laptop or desktop computer."

"I'll get it." Maddie hurried to the kitchen where Janie left her school backpack. After checking to verify the laptop was inside, she carried the entire bag into the living room and handed it to the detective.

"Thanks," he said. "We'll look into the information you gave us. What's the best number where we can reach you? And where's your shop located, in case we need to get a hold of you?" He passed her his pad and pen.

Maddie scribbled down the information he asked for and returned the pad to him. "We open the store at 9:00 am, but I'll probably open around 10:00 tomorrow since this night has been so crazy." She didn't know how she'd do it, do something so mundane as go to work while her sister was missing, but she couldn't imagine doing nothing while she waited for word. And she couldn't stay all day in the house where her sister had been attacked. "If you hear anything about my sister, will you call me right away?"

Derek ran his hand through his hair again. "I'll personally call you if we discover anything. If you think of additional information, here's my card. Don't hesitate to call me at any time. Sometimes, the smallest details turn out to be the most important."

She nodded as she took the card. "I'm glad you're on the case, Derek."

He frowned. "This place is now a crime scene. Do you have somewhere else you can go? And do you need help gathering some things to take with you?"

Maddie shook her head automatically, although she hadn't thought that far ahead. "Do I have to leave? I have LouLou. It's difficult to find dog-friendly accommodations. Can't I stay here?"

"You might be able to stay if we cordon off Janie's room, but what if the attacker returns?" Derek's frown deepened. "You said yourself LouLou wasn't a guard dog."

"I can't leave the house," Maddie explained. "What if Janie returns?"

"I'll have a uniform drive by several times through the remainder of the night."

"Thanks," she said.

"I'm sorry about your sister," he said, his tone gentle, his gaze sincere. "We'll do everything we can to find her." He lifted her hand and squeezed it.

Warmth spread up her arm and through her body, heating her all over. Then he was gone.

When the other officers left, Maddie locked the doors behind them and pulled out her phone.

Time to call Dad.

ABOUT PAIGE YANCEY

PAIGE YANCEY is the daughter of New York Times Bestselling Author Elle James. She's a wife, a mother of two wonderful boys and a nurse. She gets her love of reading from her mother and grandmother. Since she was a teenager, she's been brainstorming ideas with her mother, helping her to dream up stories for her readers. She's excited to debut her third book in her mother's Brotherhood Protector's World. Paige loves to hear from her readers. You can write to her at paigeyanceyauthor@gmail.com

facebook.com/paige.yancey.710

ORIGINAL BROTHERHOOD PROTECTORS SERIES

BY ELLE JAMES

ABOUT ELLE JAMES

ELLE JAMES also writing as MYLA JACKSON is a *New York Times* and *USA Today* Bestselling author of books including cowboys, intrigues and paranormal adventures that keep her readers on the edges of their seats. With over eighty works in a variety of sub-genres and lengths she has published with Harlequin, Samhain, Ellora's Cave, Kensington, Cleis Press, and Avon. When she's not at her computer, she's traveling, snow skiing, boating, or riding her ATV, dreaming up new stories. Learn more about Elle James at www.ellejames.com

Website | Facebook | Twitter | GoodReads | Newsletter | BookBub | Amazon

Follow Elle!
www.ellejames.com
ellejames@ellejames.com

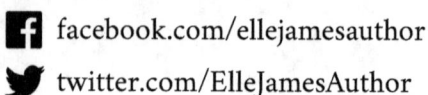

facebook.com/ellejamesauthor

twitter.com/ElleJamesAuthor